Castle of Shadows

~ Tales of Karensa ~

Jean Cullop

Scripture Union

By the same author
Tales of Karensa: Where Dolphins race with Rainbows

Copyright © Jean Cullop
First published 2001

Scripture Union, 207–209 Queensway, Bletchley,
Milton Keynes, MK2 2EB, England.

ISBN 1 85999 463 6

All rights reserved. No part of this publication may be
reproduced, stored in a retrieval system, or transmitted in
any form or by any means, electronic, mechanical,
photocopying, recording or otherwise, without the prior
permission of Scripture Union.

The right of Jean Cullop to be identified as author of this
work has been asserted by her in accordance with the
Copyright, Designs and Patents Act 1988.

British Library Cataloguing-in-Publication Data.
A catalogue record of this book is available from the British
Library.

Printed and bound in Great Britain by Creative Print and
Design (Wales) Ebbw Vale.

Contents

The Lost Kingdom

As far away as yesterday is an island called Karensa, where dolphins race with rainbows and woodland creatures walk freely in the Dark Forest, and broken hearts are healed.

The people of Karensa had lived and spoken in ways unchanging since ancient times and each one could go to the King, who met every need with perfect love and justice.

Then came the Day of Sorrow when Lord Bellum disobeyed the King and for that he was cast out of the Royal Palace. Fear was born on Karensa, and the way to the King was closed. Lord Bellum built his own castle, for he was determined that one day he, not the King, would be ruler of Karensa, and many people believed the false promises he made.

The King's word decreed that the punishment for disobedience was death, and the King would not put his own desires above the truth of his word. His people must die.

Yet this King loved his people more than they would ever know, and in love sent his son, Salvis, to die in their place, although his own heart was broken.

So it was at the very moment Salvis died, all those who were held captive in Bellum's castle were set free and defeat was turned into a great victory.

Salvis now lives again in the Royal Palace and to all who put their trust in him, he gives forgiveness and the King's power. This means that the people may once again approach the King, who will hear them call even from the silence of their hearts.

So it will be on Karensa until the day that Salvis rides out from the Palace and claims back the Lost Kingdom.

The Butterflies' Song

Beyond the cool trees of the great, Dark Forest,
And the Meadow of Flowers, green and fair,
A song is heard in the Castle of Shadows,
Music of sorrows,
Of lost tomorrows,
From butterflies imprisoned there.

Carried on gentle evening breezes,
The sound of their fragile, fluttering wings.
Soften your heart, be still and listen.
Music of sorrows,
Of lost tomorrows,
A cloud of butterflies softly sings.

Fisher village

Luke and Rosie
arrived here

Harbour

Farmland

Tobias
farm

High
Hill

Dark Forest

Narrow track

Black Rock
Bay

Carrik's
house

road

Fields

Dark Forest

King's
Palace

Coastal path

Ford

Bellum's
Castle

Stream

River

Kett's house

Meadow
of
Flowers

Moors

Bay of
Dolphins

Farms

The far side of the island

Town

Farms

Bay of
Perils

Karensa

Chapter 1

The Meadow of Flowers

Morwen was paddling. She had rolled up the legs of her trousers and she was splashing in the ice cold water of the stream.

It was the warmest day she could ever remember in the whole of her twelve years. She had turned up the sleeves of her tunic so that her freckled arms were bare. Her red-gold hair was braided and wound around her head to keep her neck cool.

"Come in, Petroc!" she called to her brother, screwing up her light green eyes against the sun. "The water is so cold! It will cool you down!"

Thirteen-year-old Petroc shook his head. He was sitting comfortably in a shady spot he had found, and replied that he was too lazy to move. The water did look good. The clear stream chattered happily through the Meadow of Flowers from the Dark Forest into the very heart of Karensa.

The truth was, Petroc was embarrassed. For nearly a year, all through the war, his loyalty to the King had kept him a prisoner in Bellum's evil stronghold, forced to work for the cruel Lord Carrik, Bellum's highest servant and also the King's enemy. His captivity had left him weak and thin so, although he was still tall, the rest of him had become thin and wasted. He had no intention of revealing his white, spindly legs to Morwen or to anyone else.

So he sat where he was, hot and tired, and continued to look out towards the sea.

Morwen looked at him and sighed inwardly. She knew how unhappy her brother was, and she felt guilty that she could not share his sadness, but today the world felt good. The sky was blue and the sun was hot and the grass was strewn with wild flowers of every colour. Their scent was heavy on the breeze.

She splashed her way through the crystal clear water, up and down the stream until at last she grew tired and sat down by Petroc's side.

"You seem so sad," she ventured. "Is it because Lord Salvis has returned to the Royal Palace?"

"Salvis!" Petroc's voice rose angrily. "No, not Salvis!"

"Then it must be because Luke and Rosie have gone home."

Petroc's face was expressionless. He had the same red hair and green eyes as his sister but where she bubbled with life, his eyes were dull and his pale, drawn face seemed defeated and without purpose.

As usual, Morwen had been right. Petroc was thinking of their two friends, Luke and Rosie, who had been visitors from the world beyond the mist.* He did miss them. His one thought during all those months when he had been forced to live in Bellum's stronghold, was to escape and rejoin his family and friends. It was the only thing that had given him hope when he felt all else was hopeless. He and

---

* Their story is told in *Where Dolphins race with Rainbows*

Luke had become closer than brothers, in spite of their different worlds. Or maybe because of them? Petroc had never known anyone so well as Luke.

When at last Petroc was set free, Salvis had decided that it was time for Luke and Rosie to go home.

Morwen placed her hand over her brother's hand, her hand freckled and brown, his wasted and pale. Her hand was cool from the stream.

"I miss them too, brother," she said gently. "Especially... especially Luke... Luke was special to me, but... they had to go home... Their world is not our world..."

"It has been two days since they left. Do you think they are home yet?"

"Of course they are! The dolphins who guided them have returned and are playing in the deep waters off the Bay. Oh, Petroc, I know we shall see them again one day! And... and... I miss Lord Salvis, too... I do not think there was ever anyone like him, ever before."

"Salvis, Salvis, that is all I hear! What do you know, Morwen? You know nothing! You cannot even begin to imagine what Bellum is really like! Do you think it was easy, being made to serve him? And what did Salvis do? Nothing at all! He didn't even put up a fight!"

"When he died you were set free."

"He didn't die! How could he have really died? He was standing talking to us on the beach a few days later!"

By now tears were trickling down Morwen's face.

"He did die, Petroc. You know it. You saw it happen," she sobbed.

"Then it must have been a trick."

"You know it was was not. You know it was real. Oh Petroc, you have changed! Once you would never have spoken so."

Petroc looked away from her. Even in his present mood he was sorry to have made her cry.

Once more she was right. Once there had been no war on Karensa. Once the King had ruled with perfect justice and taken care of all his people's problems.

Once it had been right for Petroc to obey his father, Tobias, but now Tobias was dead, killed by Carrik, their landlord, whom Petroc had been forced to serve.

Once... once he and Morwen had been happy, just simple farm children, loved and cared for. Now their farm was burnt to the ground.

Once he'd had plenty to eat. He had never known hunger. Now he had endured months of near starvation.

Once... once the King's servants had been pleased to serve a king who ruled with perfect justice. Now, Lord Bellum had disobeyed that King and so he had been thrown out of the Royal Palace, taking a third of the King's servants with him. Within hours of Bellum's disobedience, fear and death had come to the island of Karensa, until at last the King had sent his son, Salvis, to stand against Bellum. Salvis had lost his life and at the very moment of his death, the prisoners in Bellum's castle, including Petroc, had been set free. Now the war was over but things would never be quite the same as they were before.

From the corner of his eye, across the shallow Meadow of Flowers, Petroc could see the dark outline of Bellum's stronghold where the King's enemy still lived and ruled.

"Brother, do you realise," Morwen said suddenly, "It was at this very spot that Lord Salvis was taken prisoner on the night he died?"

"Let himself be taken, you mean. Why didn't he fight? He could easily have defeated Bellum. He had an army at his side. All those who stayed loyal to the King."

"That was not the way it had to be. Oh, Petroc, it is because you never really got to know him. You did not have time. While you were... were captured, Lord Salvis lived with us, all through the Time of Snows. If only you could have known him for yourself! He had such peace! Even when he knew he was to die he still had that peace. It feels as though he left some of his peace with his friends when he died."

Abruptly, Petroc stood up and turned his back on her. As he turned his back, he closed his heart.

Morwen rolled down the legs of her trousers and eased her feet into her soft boots. It seemed wrong that anyone should be sad on such a day. The Time of Plenty was too short on Karensa. Soon enough the Time of Gathering would be here, only this year they had no harvest to gather; they did not have a farm any more. Not for the first time Morwen wondered what their future would be.

They were still living in a cave house in the Bay of Dolphins, but they could not stay there for ever. She supposed decisions would soon have to be made about their future. She pushed such thoughts right from her mind. Petroc was unhappy. She was sad because she missed Luke and Rosie and Lord Salvis. Yet she was not going to let anything spoil such a perfect day.

Chapter 2

Words of Ancient Days

From the highest window of the Royal Palace, the King and his son could see over the entire kingdom of Karensa.

The King bowed to his son, and as he moved his head, the jewels in his crown reflected bright colours on his royal robes of purple and gold.

His son's head was bare, and he was dressed in a simple grey tunic and loose fitting trousers, but the power surrounding him revealed that he was indeed the son of a great king and that his peasant clothes meant nothing.

Above them, the golden turrets and silver pennants of the Palace shimmered; below them, the island of Karensa basked peacefully in the morning sunshine. The war was over. Victory was being proclaimed throughout the land.

"Welcome home, Salvis," said the King. "My son, I am well pleased. You were obedient to my word even to death."

Salvis inclined his head so that his light brown hair fell across his face.

"Father, you know that it was for this purpose that I was born," he said simply.

"Ah yes, my son, but I did not force you to obey me. It was your decision. You could have refused."

"Then the people would never have been able to

15

enter the Royal Palace again, for that is what your word decreed."

"Salvis, my word is higher than all things, even my own desires. When my people turned away from me, I could no longer allow them inside the Palace walls, because their disobedience would have put an end to my perfect justice. You alone were obedient and you were willing to die in their place. You took the punishment that should have been theirs. You died instead of them, although you were innocent of any crime. Now I give you back your life for ever and you shall receive the highest honour."

"So the war is ended, Father?"

The King sighed. "No, it is not ended, Salvis. Our enemy Bellum still lives in his castle on the far side of the Dark Forest, just beyond the Meadow of Flowers. His castle is fast becoming a mighty stronghold. Many will listen to Bellum. The war has only just begun."

The King and Salvis stood silently considering these things, for they both loved the people of Karensa with a love that went beyond sacrifice.

They were joined by the King's most loyal and faithful servant, Veritan, Lord of the Palace. He was almost as splendid as the King, with a jewelled circlet over his long silver hair, and precious gems shining from his belt and from the hilt of his golden sword.

"All seems well, Lord King."

Once again the King sighed, an eternal sigh for all the world's deep sorrows.

"There is much to accomplish before Bellum is finally defeated and Karensa is ours once more.

Even today, Veritan, I am sending you out with work to do."

"Anything, Lord King... but..." Veritan hesitated.

"Speak your mind," commanded the King. "You need have no fear of me, Veritan. You have been faithful to me in all things."

"It is only... Lord King... why not be done with Bellum now, once and for ever? Why not simply end his power?"

The King looked down across the sunlit island and beyond to where the mist obscured the horizon. Karensa was always surrounded by this mist. It rarely cleared.

The King's face became thoughtful and sad.

"Bellum... Bellum once loved me," he said at last, choosing his words with great care. "Remember the music he made for us in the time before the war? Such music led my people to worship me, but then... yet that is not the reason... There are many people on Karensa who wish to come into the Royal Palace and who would love the old laws to return. They have the right to choose between Bellum and my word."

"But, Lord King... you are all powerful and Salvis, too, has your power, the very power of creation. Bellum is nothing. He turned your people against you. He is a liar... a deceiver... a serpent... nothing at all..."

"Bellum has all the power my people are willing to give him. No less, no more. I will not permit anyone to take authority above my word. One day Salvis will cast Bellum from Karensa, never to return. Until then the battle goes on. Now let us rejoice as we welcome my son home."

* * *

At one end of the Great Hall, on a high platform, stood three marble thrones. On both sides of the hall the King's servants were assembled, each one dressed in shining white. The pure brightness of their robes contrasted with the many coloured banners hanging from each stone pillar. The hall was lit by a strange silver light which transformed the marble floor into a sea of moving colours.

The King led the way towards the thrones and as he did so, Salvis changed. His robes became dazzling white, and as he walked further and further towards the thrones, his face began to shine with the radiance of a thousand suns, and to reflect the quiet peace of a thousand moons. Even in his brilliance, all servants who had true hearts could look upon Salvis without fear, for although his eyes flashed fire, it was a fire born of the greatest love in all creation.

The King commanded Salvis to kneel and he placed a crown on his son's head, a crown that sent rays of light in every direction so that it was never still.

Then at last Salvis took his place at the right hand of the King. A mighty shout of joy and triumph arose as each servant began to praise the King in words older than time and sweeter than tomorrow's dawn, secret words of ancient days, words of power and great beauty, never before spoken and now carved into eternity.

The King and Salvis took their seats, and with them, the presence of an Unseen Lord fell upon the third throne. All three thrones, although separate, were One, as they always had been and as they always would be. The Three were One and yet were Three. It was the Deep Secret of Creation.

The King gave a loud cry, a heart cry full of love and victory, a cry that resounded through the entire universe.

"Now, my son who was dead is alive again! Now my people can come to me once more! Now, Salvis, you wear your royal robes. You made yourself lower than the least of my people. You accepted the worst that Bellum could do and did not once falter or turn away from me or the work I had given to you. One day you will judge the people of Karensa and from now onward all those who trust in you will be welcomed into the Royal Palace. Meanwhile, let the battle continue. Salvis has already won the final victory, but the spoils of war have yet to be divided. Now my people must choose whom they will follow, and Bellum will try everything in his power to keep them from coming to me, for he desires only that they should worship him, and he is a cunning adversary. My friends, this is where the real conflict starts."

Veritan lifted high the golden sword of truth and a great and mighty call to arms resounded around the Hall and was carried to the ends of the Earth.

Chapter 3

A Fallen Crown

As Morwen and Petroc sat in the sun by the stream, there was a sudden movement over by the edge of the Dark Forest. Morwen stood up, shading her green eyes against the sun. "Petroc, see, over there, butterflies! Hundreds of them!"

Coming towards them across the Meadow of Flowers, was a beautiful coloured cloud, a cloud made of fluttering wings that shimmered in the heat haze, pink and blue, purple and white, yellow, red and gold.

The cloud came nearer and to Morwen's delight the butterflies flew all around them until they were completely hidden in the moving cloud.

Butterfly wings brushed their cheeks, their lips, their eyes, their hands. They were soft as gossamer.

"Listen, Petroc, listen to their song!"

Her brother could hear nothing. He stood there with the lovely creatures fluttering all around him and he might have been made of stone.

"Butterflies do not sing, Morwen," he said flatly.

"They do! They do! They make music with their wings! I never heard such a sound! Like the breath of bells, thousands and thousands of little bells. But so sad, such sad music!" Still Petroc heard nothing. As the butterflies moved on across the Meadow of Flowers, Morwen became agitated.

"Petroc, we must stop them. They are on their way to Bellum's stronghold. We must not let them go there!"

In desperation she began to call, "Butterflies, butterflies, come back!"

The butterflies, as if drawn by a great magnet, were heading straight towards the one place they should not go.

Soon, Petroc and Morwen were once more alone. Neither of them heard the horseman until he spoke to them.

"Petroc, son of Tobias, the King told me that I should find you here."

They span round, for one moment believing that Lord Salvis had returned.

It was not Salvis but Veritan, Lord of the Royal Palace, who slid down from his grey horse.

He was an impressive figure, a giant almost, with a gold circlet over his silver hair and piercing eyes as blue as the tunic he wore. From his belt hung his golden sword, the sword that had never yet been defeated in battle, the hilt encrusted with priceless jewels.

Petroc and Morwen stood as though turned to stone, Morwen because she had no idea who this could be, and Petroc because he did know. He remembered Lord Veritan from the time he had gone to the Royal Palace with his friend, Luke. He remembered too, that Lord Veritan's loyalty to the King was unshakeable and that he, Petroc, had just been saying things that were not at all loyal.

That thought prompted him to kneel, and Morwen copied him. She still did not know who it was she knelt to and she began to tremble in fear.

"Get up, both of you," Veritan said in a voice that was both kindly and stern. "You must kneel to Salvis and to the King, but not to me. I am Veritan, Lord of the King's Palace, and his messenger today."

Quickly, they scrambled to their feet. Morwen summoned up enough courage to raise her eyes to Veritan's face. To her surprise, her fear evaporated. Petroc was not so sure. Why should the King's highest servant seek them out, if it did not mean trouble?

It was as though Veritan could read his thoughts.

"Petroc, son of Tobias," he said. "The King has sent me to look for you, as you have found much favour with him. He has known of the hardship you endured, first at the hand of Carrik, the landlord, and then by his master, Bellum. The King sees you as someone he can trust and someone deserving of reward. You remained loyal to him throughout your troubles. The King wishes to restore to you the farming land that Bellum destroyed. The King has a special purpose for your farm."

Suddenly, Petroc felt very, very tired. More than anything in the world he wanted to forget the last months and put the past behind him. He could not bring himself to even think about the future.

"The King cannot bring back my father, whom Carrik killed," he said wearily. "He cannot bring back my friends, whom Salvis sent away."

Veritan rubbed his chin with his hand, all the while staring keenly at Petroc. Then he looked away over towards the Dark Forest then again to the stronghold castle behind them. He seemed to be considering something very carefully.

"I believe there is something you must do first," he stated. "You must come with me, both of you. Come, you may ride my horse."

The horse neighed softly.

"He wants us to obey," Morwen laughed, delighted that she could sense how the horse was feeling, for she had not felt so close to the animals since Bellum had brought fear to the island by disobeying the King.

Petroc only heard a horse neighing.

Veritan helped them up, Petroc in the saddle and Morwen in front of him, holding tightly onto the horse's neck as Veritan walked beside them, leading them on. It seemed strange that the King's highest servant had given up his horse to peasant children.

"Where are we going, Lord?" Morwen ventured. She hoped it would be to the Royal Palace. She wanted so much to see Salvis again. She wanted it so much that it was like a real pain, deep inside.

"No," Veritan told her sadly. "One day, child you will meet Salvis again, but he will never be as he was before, and that will not be today. Today we have somewhere else to go and it is in the opposite direction. I am taking you to Bellum's stronghold castle."

"No!" The words left Petroc's lips before he could stop them. "No... no, Lord, I cannot go back there!"

His cry disturbed the horse, who faltered briefly and then recovered beneath Veritan's restraining hand.

"Yes you can, Petroc," Veritan said firmly and

the strength in his voice reminded them that he was there as the King's messenger and the King must be obeyed. "You will come with me to the very camp of the enemy. Bellum has no power over you any more. You have been set free. You must prove it to yourself. You must learn to trust the King."

Petroc thought, and you have no idea what Bellum is really like. I do. I know him very well.

The stronghold was even darker than Petroc remembered and as he and Morwen climbed down from Veritan's horse, the boy shivered with sudden fear. It was only a few days since he had been set free, and even in that time the walls of the castle seemed even more forbidding.

On the other hand Bellum, who met them at the gate to the castle, looked magnificent. Salvis' death had gone to Bellum's head – literally – for now his black hair carried a crown. It seemed strange, but the gold in the crown was dull, and the jewels did not shine. It was like a poor shadow of the King's crown.

Bellum also carried a sword of black steel. His tunic was black too, and edged with gold.

Veritan and Bellum stood face to face, two giants in the kingdom of Karensa. As their eyes met it was as though lightning pierced the air. The children each gave a shiver of excitement and fear. They were fascinated yet at the same time afraid.

Quite suddenly Bellum laughed. It was unexpected and unnerving.

"So you have come to join me, Veritan!" he roared. "Now that Salvis is dead you will need someone to serve."

"I will never serve you, Bellum, you know that full well." Veritan's voice was as cold as the ice that formed in the Dark Forest during the Time of Snows. "Salvis is not dead. He lives, and has gone to take his rightful place in the Royal Palace. Even now, he sits at his Father, the King's side."

Bellum continued to laugh. "Of course he is dead!" He took the black sword from its scabbard. "See, my sword still carries his blood!"

Morwen felt hot tears sting her eyes as she saw that the blade of Bellum's sword was stained dark red for she knew in her spirit that Bellum was telling the truth and that this really was Salvis' own lifeblood that was shed when he died.

Yet, as they watched, something unbelievable happened. The red stain faded and disappeared from the blade of the sword.

The children gasped. Veritan smiled triumphantly.

"See, Bellum, Salvis is no longer dead. It is as I told you. He lives again in the Royal Palace!"

Bellum's eyes changed from black to amber in fury as he realised that Veritan was telling the truth. He glared at his sword. His face darkened. In his expression they sensed each terror of the longest night, each unspoken fear of mankind, fears past and fears to come, fears not yet created. His voice became that of the hissing serpent he had taken as his heraldic emblem.

"So, the war goes on. Yet I will still be the ruler of this island. It will be to me that the people of Karensa will turn."

Petroc and Morwen clung together in fear as the air was suddenly rent by a great crash of thunder.

The thunder rumbled again and again, but it was not like any thunder they had ever heard before. This was thunder born of the fury of creation.

The ground shook violently. Wind rushed across the Meadow of Flowers, flattening wild flowers and grasses. Trees bent low as if bowing before an unseen force. The sky grew dark. Then, with a mighty rush of wind, Bellum's crown was torn from his head and rolled away into the long grass, faster and faster, through the Meadow of Flowers.

Then it was quiet. The sun shone once again and the sky was blue.

"Find the crown!" Bellum roared across the still meadow, only now his voice was edged with a deep fear which he was desperately trying to hide.

Petroc and Morwen moved to obey him, but Veritan pulled them back as the crown disappeared into the long grass.

"Your power is broken, Bellum," Veritan laughed. "Did you really think that the King would stand by and let you take his kingdom from him?"

"You will see my power! You will all see! You, boy, Petroc, I remember you. Why have you come here? Can it be that you have come home?"

To Petroc's dismay his knees began to shake, and the more he tried to stop them, the more they trembled. His tongue clung to the roof of his mouth.

Morwen replied for him. "This is not his home! This was never his home!"

Bellum sneered. "Your sister speaks in your place. Yet I recall you were not weak when you served Carrik in my stronghold. You were stubborn then, and proud. It gave us much sport to try to break your spirit, but we never did. Do you recall the night we told you how your father died? Ah, I see that you do..."

By now, Petroc was shaking visibly and hating himself for it. Morwen was staring at him, silently pleading with him to find his courage. "You did not!" he blurted at last. "You did not break me, Lord Bellum!"

"No, no, we did not..." Bellum narrowed his eyes. His voice became a whisper. "Petroc, come back now. Come back with me inside the castle. I need someone like you to be at my side. Soon you will be a man. Then I will give you treasure beyond your dreams. See, my gates are never locked or barred. You can come and go at any time. I do not stop people coming to me as the King has done. Come back now. Not as a servant, Petroc. Not as a prisoner. Come now of your own free will. When you are a man you will walk beside me. When Karensa is really mine, you will share my glory. The people will bow down to me. They will worship me. They will wonder at my splendour and marvel at my music. Oh, Petroc, such music... you have heard the music I can make."

He paused for breath.

"This will never be," Veritan declared resolutely. Bellum ignored him. It was doubtful he even heard him.

"What do you say, boy? You will not have to work. You will never have to dig and plough. And your sister too. She has a fair face. I will give her fine clothes to wear. I will teach her to make music, and to dance."

His gaze made Morwen feel embarrassed. Then suddenly a picture of Salvis came into her mind and she forgot her shyness and found her courage again.

"I won't," she cried. "I won't be there. I won't ever go inside your castle!"

"Oh yes you will, Morwen." Bellum smiled lazily, still gazing at her in the same way. "One day, of your own free will, you will walk inside those gates. So will many more. The people want to live their own lives. They do not always want to be bound by the King's laws. His time is ended here."

Lord Veritan's hand reached for his sword. Then, as if thinking better of it, he let it rest.

"Your power comes from mankind's fear of death and our Lord Salvis has overcome death on Karensa for ever," Veritan stated.

Bellum gave a short laugh. "Let the people choose then: pleasure now, or hardship and promises. They will choose pleasure every time. Look at this boy," he pointed a ringed finger at Petroc. "He may seem to be free but in his heart he still belongs in my stronghold." With that he turned abruptly and went back inside. They heard him shouting to servants to find his lost crown.

Morwen felt for her brother's hand and held it tight. "You are free, Petroc. Don't believe what Bellum says," she whispered.

"He is a liar," Veritan agreed. "One day he will be known as the Father of Lies."

Petroc made a big effort and stopped trembling but he was still shaking inside. He was scared. Losing his nerve was something he had never experienced before.

As Bellum's servants ran out to search for the fallen crown, Veritan helped the children back onto his horse.

They walked away, glad to see the back of the dark Castle of Shadows, and Veritan talked to them.

"The King sent me to help you, Petroc. He wants you to go back to your farm. He has issued a just decree that all lands destroyed by Bellum must be given back to the tenant farmers. You will never have to pay rent to your landlord, Carrik, again. The farm will be yours."

A flicker of interest shone from Petroc's green eyes. Then, "Yes, but... there is only me, Lord. And Morwen and my mother. Oh, and Delfi, but she is only very small. Farming is hard. We need a grown man to help us with the work."

Veritan laughed softly. "Oh, Petroc, do not say 'yes, but' to the King. The King has the answer to all things and the King will provide. Come, I will take you back through the Dark Forest."

The horse neighed softly as they crossed the Meadow of Flowers.

More butterflies were flying towards Bellum's castle and Morwen could not resist looking back over her shoulder.

She began to wonder what the castle was really like inside.

Chapter 4

Amos

The sudden burst of bright light hurt their eyes as they left the dappled shade of the Dark Forest. Before them was the Bay of Dolphins, or the Bay of Peace as it had been called since Salvis had lived there. It shimmered and sparkled in the hot afternoon sun.

Morwen said suddenly, "I wonder if Bellum has found his crown?"

"He will never find it, no matter how hard he searches," Veritan replied. "Now, I must return to the Royal Palace, but before I go I believe the King has a message for each of you." He placed his hand on Morwen's shoulder. "Child, do not let your curiosity destroy your faithfulness. Remember that loyalty to the King is the only way that leads to lasting peace." Next he turned to Petroc. "And you, no longer a child yet not a man, learn to trust the King. The way to overcome fear is to face it and that is what you have done by going to Bellum's castle."

"Yes, but... I was afraid," said Petroc, biting his lip.

"Only a fool has no fear," Veritan smiled. "You did not run away, although you wanted to. You stood your ground. When you did that Bellum could not touch you. Remember that in the days ahead."

Petroc nodded. He was feeling better about himself already.

Veritan stroked his horse and then leapt swiftly and easily on to its back.

"I am only the King's messenger. He has a special task for both of you to do and he will provide the means to do it. The King is aware of how loyal your family has been, how faithful to his laws. Be confident that the King will help you."

He raised his hand in a gesture of farewell, turned, and in an instant he was riding like the wind through the Dark Forest.

Petroc and Morwen stared at each other.

Morwen spoke first. "Why us, brother? Why did such an important person come to see us?"

Petroc had no answer to give, as he had been asking himself the very same question. "Let's not go straight home," he said instead. "Let's go down to the beach. It will be cooler by the sea, sitting on the rocks." He did not add that it was there they had last seen Salvis, before he went back to the Royal Palace.

They climbed down the steep cliff path to the flat rock where they could look out to sea.

"Petroc, why is there always a mist around the island?"

Once again she had taken him by surprise. In the old days Morwen would never have thought to ask such questions. Now they seemed to pop out without warning, like a cork from a bottle.

"Father used to say Karensa was a special place," he said slowly. "He said it was a place that only a few people found, and that is why not many visitors come here."

"But I wish... I wish we could see what is on the other side of the mist. We did, just once, and there was land, not too far away. If we had a boat we could sail through the mist and see what is on the other side."

"Why should we want to do that?" It had never occurred to Petroc to live anywhere but Karensa.

"I don't know, I suppose I was thinking of Rosie and Luke. Petroc, what did Bellum mean, about how they told you Father had died?"

"You are best not to know," he told her abruptly. "Anyway, I don't remember."

"Yes, you do."

"I don't! Stop asking so many questions! I do not want to remember, Morwen!"

Morwen did not press him, but a stubborn streak in her made her resolve that somehow, she would find out. But not today.

"Oh, Petroc, don't let us be sad and argue, not today. It has been such a day! And it is wonderful that you are back home again!"

Petroc hardened his heart.

"You go and look for shells," he said. He wanted time on his own. It was one of the things his long captivity had not allowed.

Morwen understood and went off quite gladly on her own.

However, it was not cooler on the beach. If anything it was even hotter, so, forgetting his pride, Petroc pulled off his boots, rolled up his trousers and paddled in the sea. The water was wonderfully cold. The waves, lapping gently against his bare legs, were calming. People were right to call this the

Bay of Peace. It was almost as if he could still feel Salvis here, as cool and as calm as the sea was now.

Then, quite unexpectedly he too began to wonder what lay beyond the mist. He had never wondered before. Karensa was his home and Karensa had always been surrounded by mist. That was how things were. He had accepted it. But now after meeting Luke and Rosie he was curious about other lands.

He thought of his father. Tobias was a good man. He would have been pleased if they really could restore the farm. Yet how would they? His mother was old now and could no longer work in the fields. They had a child called Delfi staying with them who his mother seemed to have taken under her wing, but Delfi was too little. He and Morwen could never do all the work on their own.

Besides, he was not at all sure that he wanted Salvis or the King to help him. In Bellum's stronghold they had heard of Salvis and the army he was gathering in the Bay of Dolphins. They had all dreamed of the day when Salvis would rise to fight Bellum and put him to the sword.

Sadly, it had not gone that way. It was Salvis who had died and once he had been captured, his great army had run away.

Morwen lay on her stomach and leant over a rock pool. In the still water she could see her reflection as clear as any mirror. She studied herself with a critical eye. She saw an oval face sprinkled with freckles and surrounded by a coronet of red-gold hair, light green eyes, a small, neat nose and a mouth that was both full and wide. With a sudden shock she realised that Bellum had been right. She was pretty.

Almost at once a picture of Salvis came into her mind. Her heart missed a beat. She sprang to her feet.

"Petroc! I'm going home! Mother will want me to help with the meal!"

Martha did not need her daughter's help after all, because the meal was ready. All that was needed on such a hot day was cold meat, cheese, crusty brown bread and fruit, all of which were plentiful.

Petroc blinked against the sudden darkness of the cave house. He was still weak. The hard climb up the cliff steps had left him breathless. Thankfully, he sank down at the wooden table, trying to hide how out of breath he was. It was only then that they both realised they had a visitor.

"Uncle Amos!" Morwen threw herself at him, suddenly a child again. "What brings you here?"

The big, red-headed, red-bearded man laughed loudly. Everything Amos did was loud. "Maiden you grow too old for such behaviour!" he exclaimed. "Why, you've taken the air clear out of my chest! Stand back now so I may look at you, for I think you have grown tall. Soon you will be a young woman and then some young man shall come and steal you away!"

Morwen blushed. "Uncle! I am only twelve," she protested, but not before she thought of Luke. She had hoped one day they might be more than friends, but it seemed that this was not to be.

Amos turned his attention to Petroc and the laughter died on his lips. A sigh escaped him.

"Oh, what has happened to you, boy?"

"You know what happened, Uncle," Petroc twisted his mouth into a wry smile.

"Was Carrik so harsh to you?"

Petroc started to feel embarrassed. "Bellum was," he muttered tersely. "Look, I've left something on the beach. I'll fetch it. Don't wait for me. You start your meal."

He almost ran from the house, setting aside his tiredness in his panic to get away, and ignoring Martha's call to him to return.

Amos placed his hand on Morwen's arm.

"Leave him. I was thoughtless in what I said, but it was the shock of seeing him so... so thin and pale. In a moment I shall seek him out and put things right. No, better still, I shall go now."

He hurried out after Petroc. They heard his voice bellowing across the beach and exchanged sighs for they both thought that Petroc needed peace and quiet.

Not for the first time, Morwen noticed that her mother looked very tired. Her hair, once red, was now grey. The brown tunic and trousers that she wore hung loosely from her shoulders; for once she had been plump and now she was thin.

"Mother," she hesitated. "Mother, you are not ill, are you?"

Martha sighed. "I don't know, child. At times it seems that all my energy is spent. Still," she gestured to the dark haired child who rarely left her side. "I have Delfi here. She is a great comfort to me."

"I try to be," the little girl said shyly. "You took me in when no one else would have me... after my father left..."

Neither Martha nor Morwen were cruel enough to say that Delfi's father, Josh, had not simply left. He had betrayed Salvis and run away and had not been seen since.

"There, my lamb, it was not your doing," Martha said softly.

Morwen sat down in the chair her brother had just left.

"Mother, why is Uncle Amos here?"

"He has an idea to put to us. He has come all the way from his home on the far side of the island with great plans, but he shall tell you of them when he returns. It may mean we have to leave here."

Morwen looked around. It was a poor enough place, but the house built in a cave had been their home for more than half a year. It was basic, only a front and back built on the cave. They had slept on straw and furs and no matter how much they washed they always seemed to smell of fish and seaweed, but it was safe. None could attack them here. Not Bellum, not Carrik, not anyone. It had been their safe house after Tobias had died.

"Mother, Delfi, you would never believe what happened today," she said. She told them all about Veritan and Bellum and all the things that had been said.

Martha listened intently, sometimes nodding, sometimes exclaiming her disbelief.

"You should keep away from that Lord Bellum and his ideas," was her only comment. "No good shall ever come of talking to that one. As for the rest of it, I think you will be surprised when you hear what your Uncle Amos has to say."

Delfi tugged at Martha's sleeve. "I think... I think Petroc misses Rosie and Luke."

"Yes, he does," Martha replied. "I am going to tell you two a secret, but you must promise not to tell a soul."

"We promise," they chorused eagerly.

"Well, I once went to see the King."

"Mother, when? You never said."

"No, well, it was a secret. It was before our last Time of Gathering. I went for Petroc."

"Why?"

"Now this is a secret, mind? I had the notion that maybe Petroc was lonely, that he needed a friend. He was always so busy helping his father that he had no time to make friends. So I went to the King and asked for a friend for my son. Then, a little while later, Rosie and Luke came to stay."

Morwen gasped. "That must be why the King sent them to live in our home?"

"I think partly that, partly for other reasons. But it did mean that Petroc found a friend."

"Is that why Petroc misses them so much now?" Delfi asked.

"I suppose it could be. But we have to remember that it is all part of the King's great plan for everyone... Now, Uncle Amos and Petroc are coming back. A secret, remember? Not a word. You must never give a secret away when someone has trusted it to you." A dark head and a red head nodded in agreement, but the girls could not resist exchanging meaningful nudges when the boy walked through the door.

Petroc hardly noticed them as he sat down near Morwen, for he seemed to have found a new energy. His eyes were bright with an excitement he could not hide.

"Mother, Uncle Amos has told me why he is here. He has come to help us restore our farm!"

Morwen's heart began to thump so loudly that she wondered if the others would hear it. She could almost see it moving beneath her tunic.

She gave a cry. Only this very day, Veritan had promised that the King would help them, and neither of them had really believed him. Now it seemed that help was here.

Chapter 5

Memories and Plans

The early morning air smelled of new life, of gulls and fish and seaweed and of the mist that hung low over the bay, but Petroc and Morwen had no time to linger on the beach. They had a long way to go, and strode off purposefully in the direction of their farm which was a good two hours' walk away.

Last night there had been a long discussion about whether or not they should be allowed to go on their own. Amos thought that he should go with them, but Martha had finally convinced him that this was something the children needed to do on their own.

Neither of them had been home since Tobias had died. If nothing else, they needed to visit his grave.

They took the coastal path. Sometimes the sea was in view and at other times it was hidden behind houses and trees. As the sun grew high in the sky the mist rolled back to the horizon and once more the air grew warm.

For the most part they walked in silence, each lost in their own memories. It was only when they paused on a grassy cliff to eat that Morwen dared to voice her thoughts.

"It all seems so long ago... Father, the farm, the visitors. We have not been home for so long. Will it still look the same?"

"I don't know... Not if Bellum set fire to it as they said."

"So what do we do then?"

"We build it again," Petroc replied steadily. "Our father's grandfather built that farm from nothing. That is what we shall do. What our great grandfather could do, we can do also."

"Yes, but times were different then. Karensa was still loyal to the King. He still dealt with people's problems each night at the Time of Decisions. The ground was rich. Now, I hear tell, there are many stones and thistles which choke the corn."

"Stones can be removed. Thistles can be pulled up. Rebuild the farm. That is what we have to do."

Morwen considered. "Well... Lord Veritan did say it was what the King wanted us to do..."

"Not for the King! Not for Veritan. Not for Salvis, either," her brother replied. "We shall do this for Father."

"What did Uncle Amos say to you, Petroc?"

Petroc stared out to sea. "He said that he is here for Mother. The war did not really touch the far side of the island where he lives, but he knew of course, that Father had been killed and the farm destroyed. Now that the war is over and all the lost lands are restored to the tenants, well then, Uncle Amos knew that getting our farm started again was the right thing to do. Our cousins are old enough to take care of Amos' own farm while he is away. That's it, really."

"Maybe the King..."

"Oh, the King, the King," Petroc was getting annoyed again. "Listen, Morwen, Uncle Amos said other things. He said that on the far side of the island they live to help each other and do not think too much about Salvis or Bellum or even the King. They help each other in need." He lowered his voice to almost a whisper. "Morwen, all I know is that our father, Tobias, was a good, kind man. He took care of us and he provided for us and... and he loved us. He would want us to start the farm again. So we do this for him... Morwen, forget all about Salvis and I shall try to forget Bellum and Carrik and all the bad things that happened to me. We shall make a new start. This last year has changed both of us. We have had to stop being children and grow up. I know I have changed..."

"Yes, you have! You were never so hard of heart before!"

"And you, too, have changed. Once you were shy and obedient. Now you are bold."

She seemed surprised. "Am I?"

"Oh, yes, sister, you are. Look at the way you spoke up to Bellum. You would never have done that a year ago. And yes, you are right, I have grown hard. We have to face life as it really is. We have enough food and money put by to last us through to this time next year, but then we shall need to reap our own harvest. Mother grows more frail. Think of the years she worked with Father out in the fields or got up before dawn to milk the cows. We owe it to her and Father to rebuild the farm."

Morwen could find no argument against that.

"Come then, brother. Pack away the rest of the meal. As always, Mother has given plenty. Do you want a last drink of water before I put it away?"

"No, save it. Let's not waste any more time."

It was much, much worse than they had imagined. All that remained of the farmhouse was a stone shell, blackened by fire, over which ivy crept at random. The roof had gone completely. The only part left intact was the outside barn.

Silently they approached the place where the door used to be. There, to the left of the building, was a grassy mound of earth. At one end someone had placed two sticks tied together to form a cross. They knew, without doubt, that this was their father's grave.

Petroc bent down and touched the wooden cross.

"What is this... this... thing here for?"

"No, leave it!" she said quickly. "Look, it has been tied with a red ribbon. That was Rosie's ribbon. She must have put it here for a purpose."

"But what does it mean?"

"I don't know. I think it has something to do with Salvis. Oh leave it, Petroc, please!"

He shrugged. He was not really bothered either way.

For a long time they stood together just looking at the grave, each with their own memories of their father and the life they had once loved. Neither of them cried. Morwen had shed all her tears when Tobias had died. Petroc had no tears inside.

He placed a thin arm about his sister's shoulders.

"Father is not here, Morwen. He's gone. That is just a body in there."

"I know," she whispered. "But I wanted to say goodbye. He was harsh sometimes, but he was a good father to us and I loved him very much. He never did anything that was not for our good. I know that now."

"So do I, and that is why we shall do his work, not because the King told us to. Or Veritan. Or Salvis."

Morwen did not agree. To her the most important thing was to obey Salvis, but she thought it wise not to say so.

A sudden noise behind them made them jump. Too late they saw the remains of their dinner disappearing in the arms of a scrawny boy.

They raced after him. He was small, so it did not take Petroc long to catch him. In no time at all, he tackled the thief and had him on the ground.

The boy lay very still. Morwen stared accusingly at Petroc.

"I didn't hurt him," Petroc cried. "Truly, Morwen, I did him no harm!"

The boy's face seemed very white. He was thin and had a mop of curly black hair.

Morwen knelt down by his side. "Oh, Petroc, it's not a boy. It's a girl. And I think she has fainted. I wonder when she last had food?"

Petroc stared. He realised it was only the girl's short hair that made him think she was a boy.

"Wait a minute, I know this girl! She... she was in Bellum's castle too. She was a prisoner, just like me. Her name is Cherry. She served a woman called Nolis. That's who cut off her hair."

"Why?" Morwen asked.

"Oh, it was the woman's brother, Tas. He admired Cherry's hair so Nolis cut it off. I do remember her."

Cherry began to moan softly.

"Quickly, get the water," Morwen ordered.

As Cherry struggled to sit up, Petroc cradled her on his lap and helped her drink from the bottle. There seemed a new tenderness about him. It was as though, at last, he had found someone who understood him.

The girl had very large, dark eyes and she stared weakly at Morwen.

"Are you hungry?" Morwen asked. "When did you last eat?"

Cherry shook her head as if she was trying to remember and could not. Morwen gave her the remains of the bread and cheese and she devoured them greedily. Now that the rosy colour was returning to her lips and cheeks, they could see why she was called Cherry.

She twisted around to see who it was that held her.

"Petroc! You here?" she gasped.

"This is my farm, Cherry," he said firmly, but in a way that made it clear he meant her no harm. "You are on my land. And you tried to steal our food. That does not matter, you were hungry, but what are you doing on my farm?"

Morwen noted that he now said 'my' farm not 'our' farm.

Cherry sank back against him. "I had nowhere to go. When we were set free... when Salvis died... I left with the others, but I had no home to go to. I walked and walked, then I found this place. I have been living here, sleeping over there." She pointed to the barn. "Does it really matter, Petroc? After all we suffered in Bellum's castle, after all the things we saw them do, after all the times we were treated roughly and starved, does it really matter that I slept in your barn? Or that I ate your dinner and helped myself to apples from your trees? Oh yes, there are apples there. Does it matter though, Petroc? Surely what really matters is that we are free?"

He put her gently to one side and got to his feet. He did not want to be reminded of things that had happened in Bellum's castle. What was more, he did not want Morwen to know about them, either.

"I need time to think," he said thickly. "Both of you, wait for me here."

He strode away from the farm as fast as his legs would go.

Chapter 6

Cherry's Story

Cherry and Morwen stared at each other in dismay. They had both jumped to their feet when Petroc had walked away.

"We should follow him," Morwen said uncertainly.

"No, he's best alone. We should leave him."

Morwen was irritated that this girl should think that she knew Petroc better than his own sister who he had grown up with.

Cherry guessed her thoughts. "I know how he feels," she explained. "I feel it too, sometimes. Sort of panicky, like I just have to run away."

"He never used to be like that," said Morwen slowly.

"But things are not as they were. I was different too, before... before ..."

Suddenly, Morwen was curious. "Let's sit down under the trees," she suggested. "You can tell me your story and I'll tell you about me. I thought you were a boy!"

"That's my hair," Cherry replied ruefully. "Nolis cut it all off. It was shorter than this once. At least now it has started to grow again."

"Who is Nolis?"

Cherry led the way over to what had once been the orchard.

"You're limping!" Morwen cried.

"Yes. It was always so. It never bothered me before but somehow, when we went to live with Bellum, it got much worse. I can run well enough. It is when I walk slowly that it shows the most."

They found a shady spot and sat down with their backs to a large apple tree. The air was sweet with the smell of ripe fruit and the warm sun and the hum of wasps and bees.

"Tell me who Nolis is," Morwen prompted.

"Very well. I'll tell you about me and then it is your turn... My father was chief steward in a big household on the far side of the island. When I was little my life was so happy! Our master and mistress were good, kind people. They had a daughter called Zena who often looked after me when I was small. We wanted for nothing. Then, when Zena grew up she married Tas, a woodcutter. She believed herself to be in love with him, I suppose, and she would not listen to her parents when they told her she was wrong. They were not the sort of people to forbid her anything that she had set her heart on, so she went ahead with their blessing. I was given to Zena as her personal maidservant and went to live with her and Tas. He was horrible, right from the very start. He has a sister called Nolis and she hated Zena, probably because Zena is fair of face and Nolis is plain. Nolis made her life and mine as hard as she could, and Tas always took her part against poor Zena. Once Zena made herself a beautiful cloak. She spent hours sewing it. When it was finished Nolis tried to claim it for her own. It is the only time I ever saw Zena get angry. She was really upset. Tas took them both to the

King at the Time of Decisions and it was on that night that Lord Bellum started the war. We never returned to the woodcutter's cottage. We went directly with Bellum. Tas helped him chop down trees for wood to build the fortifications around his castle."

She paused for breath and then recovered herself.

"In Bellum's castle it was even worse," Cherry went on. "Tas took me away from Zena and made me work for Nolis. I was never allowed to speak to Zena again." Her voice grew very faint and she brushed away the tears that were spilling from her huge, dark eyes.

Morwen took hold of her hand. Suddenly her own problems did not seem so important. Yet there was one more thing she was burning to ask.

"Cherry, the night they told Petroc that Father had died, what did happen?"

Cherry sighed. "It was the night Carrik moved to Bellum's castle. He brought Petroc with him. There must have been some sort of trouble on the way, I do not know, something to do with the visitors from the world beyond the mist."

"Luke and Rosie?"

"That's right. I am not sure exactly what happened. They brought another prisoner but we never saw him. He was locked away, in a cell deep beneath the castle. Later, they said Bellum had him put to death."

"Kett! It must have been Kett!" The cave house they were living in had once belonged to Kett.

"I do not know," Cherry admitted. "But that night there was a feast in the Great Hall. There was singing and dancing – ah yes," her voice became bitter, "Bellum can make music sweet enough to charm a mountain of stone. But that night they were angry with Petroc. Carrik was especially angry with him. He took him to the platform at the front of the hall, where everyone could see him, and stood him there on his own. Then he called for silence. When it was fully quiet he told Petroc that his father had died and that he, Carrik, was the one who had killed him. There was nothing Petroc could do because Carrik was guarded by men with swords. Everyone laughed, for they had all drunk too much wine, and then some of them began to throw food at him and he just stood there. It was terrible. He had to stand there for hours before they let him step down. But Morwen, he did not cry! His face was very white but he never let them see him cry. Only later, in the big room where they locked up the youngest captives for the night, then I heard him weeping in the dark."

Morwen buried her face in her hands. She was sobbing, because her heart was breaking for her brother and yet at the same time she was so proud of him.

"Not once," Cherry whispered. "Not once did he betray Salvis or the King!"

"There is still time for betrayal."

The girls leapt to their feet. Neither of them had been aware of the horse approaching.

Through her tears, Morwen recognised the rider and her heart sank into her boots.

"It's Carrik! What's he doing here?" she hissed under her breath.

The thin, middle-aged man overheard and looked

mildly surprised. He turned to his companion, a youth on a grey pony, and they both laughed.

"My dear child," he said to Morwen, "Why should I not be here? This is, after all, my land."

Morwen found her courage from somewhere. "It is not your land! The King has given all captured lands back to the rightful tenants. That means it is our land!"

Morwen was desperately afraid and trying not to show it. The last time she had met Carrik he had stolen grain from the farm and then carried her brother off as his prisoner. Yet today there seemed to be nothing so fearsome about him. Maybe he had changed?

Carrik shrugged carelessly. "What does that matter? I have wealth to spare. Bellum is a generous master. You are welcome to such a meagre farm, you and your brother. I doubt you will ever make a living from it, though. Where is your brother, Petroc, by the way?"

"I do not know, and if I did, I should not tell you. Neither would Cherry."

Carrik laughed again. "Dear child, do not be so disturbed by my question. I am really not concerned. Come, Esram, we have other work to do."

The horse and pony turned and trotted off in the direction of High Hill.

The girls sank to the ground. Their knees seemed to give way beneath them. They were both trembling with fear.

"I hate that man!" Cherry cried.

"He does not seem as bad as I thought..."

"Oh, Morwen, do not be deceived. He has not

changed. And that boy, I hate him even more!"

"Who is he?"

"His name is Esram. He is Carrik's nephew. He tormented all of us children while we were prisoners and could do nothing in return. He is worse than Carrik. He hates the King and he hates Salvis and all those who serve him."

"He carried a net on his pony. What is that for?"

"You may well ask! It was his favourite pastime. He would hide and wait until one of us came along carrying food or wine then he would catch us in his net. Whatever we were carrying would be spoilt. We would be punished for spoiling it and Esram would stand and laugh."

"He sounds awful! But Cherry, they have gone towards High Hill and I don't know for sure, but that may be where Petroc has gone."

Chapter 7

Esram

Petroc had not expected High Hill to be thick with thistles. There had been no thistles before, when he had sat here with Luke, the night the war had started. Now, thistles and stones and weeds were everywhere, and this would make farming much harder than it was before.

He found a clear grassy spot and sat down with his back resting against the steep slope of the hill. Just as Petroc wanted to forget the last months, he seemed to be reminded of them more and more. Cherry was the last person he had wanted to see.

Even so, he knew they had to take care of her. They could not leave her to fend for herself, for she seemed half starved, and he had already decided that tonight she must go back to the cave house. His mother would make her welcome there. She would have enough to eat and somewhere dry to sleep.

Sitting here, he could not help but think about Luke. Where was he now? Somewhere, on the other side of the mist that surrounded Karensa, was a whole world that they knew very little about. Luke had told him strange stories of things called computers, and supper cooked in a microwave oven, whatever that was, and fast food, and televisions; of places they called schools where all the children were made to go every day; of things called cars that you sat in and they took you from place to place so you did not have to walk. Oh, and virtual reality, Luke had talked a lot about virtual reality.

Sometimes Petroc felt as though he was in virtual reality now. Part of him seemed to be here, part of him seemed to be back at the farm with his father and part of him seemed still to be with Bellum and Carrik. It was difficult to tell just what was real.

A pale pink butterfly settled on his arm and then flew away. Petroc watched it dancing from leaf to leaf. Bees were busy taking pollen from the wild flowers and there was a faint hum of insects that made him feel drowsy. He put his hands behind his head and closed his eyes so that the bright sun shone red behind his eyelids. Sleep was good. Sleep made him forget the past.

He awoke with a shock as the heavy net fell over his face. As he struggled, he felt the net being pulled tight around him so that he could not move his arms. Fear and panic rushed through him, numbing his senses. In his mind he was back in Bellum's stronghold. It was no use struggling. The net was too strong and, taken by surprise as he was, he could not escape.

"Hah! Petroc! Got you at last!"

It was the voice he hated more than any other. Esram, Carrik's nephew. He was only a year older than Petroc, yet he had caused more trouble than the whole of Carrik's household put together. The net had been his favourite sport.

Petroc looked out from beneath its folds and sure enough, the thin-faced, fair-haired figure of Esram was grinning down at him.

From a place deep inside, Petroc did what he had done so many times before when he had felt like giving up. Silently, he called for the one person he knew would help him. Without words and in his heart he cried out to the King.

At once a new energy flowed through him, and with a strength more than his own strength and with a power more than his own power, he pulled off the net and broke free.

Then he threw himself on Esram before the older boy had time to gather his thoughts together. Over and over they rolled, their faces and arms scratched by thorns and thistles and stung by nettles. Neither would give in as they rolled down the steep slope of High Hill, locked together in combat. By the time they landed at the bottom, Esram's nose was streaming with blood and Petroc had a black eye. Yet still they continued to fight, punching and kicking, until at last Carrik stepped forward to pull away Esram, and Cherry and Morwen arrived and dragged off Petroc.

The boys rested for a minute, then Petroc sprang at Esram again, all his pent-up feelings being released, and in spite of all efforts to stop them, they were once more grappling on the ground.

Morwen, watching helplessly, gasped in horror as she saw her brother take a fishing knife from his belt and hold it to the other boy's throat.

Esram's face turned white with fear, but before anyone could make a move to stop the fight, they heard another voice. "Enough! In the name of the

King, stop this!"

As they turned to see who spoke, both boys froze in horror. It was Lord Veritan who stood before them, his face pale with anger and his golden sword drawn ready for battle.

"This is not the way!" he cried. "Nothing will be gained by creating war! Petroc, put that knife away and see that you keep it for the purpose which it was made. And get up, both of you."

Carrik obviously had no intention of being over-shadowed by a Lord of the Palace. He cleared his throat. "I told you boys to stop fighting!" he said, lying to regain Veritan's respect. Without Veritan he would have been about as much use as a flea in a bowl of broth, as Martha would say.

Lord Veritan ignored him. Esram and Petroc stood up and glared at each other. Both of them had torn clothes and both were bruised and blood-stained.

Petroc did as Veritan told him and put his fishing knife back in his belt.

"You, Esram," Veritan pointed to the fair-haired youth. "Leave that net at the top of the hill and do not ever use it again. You have caused mischief enough with it. Carrik, take this boy back where he belongs."

Esram opened his mouth as if he wanted to argue, but then he seemed to change his mind. His uncle led the horse and pony forward and they mounted up.

Before turning to go, Carrik lifted his hand to Veritan in a salute.

"You serve one master, Veritan, I serve another," he said softly, almost pleasantly. "We shall see which master wins the war."

"The outcome is already decided, Carrik," Veritan replied. "All that is left is to declare our allegiance. Who is for Bellum; who is for the King?"

Carrik inclined his head. "Many will be for Bellum," he replied, but without malice. Then Carrik and Esram were gone.

"As for you, Petroc," Veritan said, "you know what you have to do. Begin the work the King has given you and he will provide all the tools you need."

He leapt on his horse and, before the children had time to ask any more questions, he too was gone.

"Well," Cherry said at last. "Just who was that?"

She was standing with her hands on her hips and her head to one side. She looked so funny, with her short, cropped hair and red cheeks, that both Petroc and Morwen burst out laughing.

Then Petroc groaned with pain for Esram had landed several hard kicks in his ribs and it hurt to laugh.

"We should go back to the farm," he murmured. "I need to sit down."

He limped back like a wounded soldier, with Morwen holding him on one side and Cherry on the other.

Thankfully he sat down in the shelter of the barn. Morwen washed his scratched face and arms, while Cherry took the wide linen belt from her tunic and bound his ribs.

Their old well was still fresh and clean and they filled a bottle and gave it to him to drink.

"Is this where you have been living, Cherry?" Morwen asked.

She nodded. "It is dry and warm. Lonely though, especially at night, when... when the..."

"When the bad dreams come," Petroc finished for her.

She nodded again.

"I have them, too," he told her. It was the first time he had admitted it to anyone. "But Cherry, you won't ever be alone again. I have made up my mind. This farm is my home. Now that my father, Tobias, is dead, I am the rightful farmer and I will not leave it again. Tonight I shall sleep here in the barn. You will go back to the Bay of Dolphins with Morwen and fetch Mother and Delfi and Uncle Amos. Then, tomorrow we shall start to rebuild our home."

Chapter 8

New Power

Petroc shivered as he pulled the rough woollen blanket around his shoulders. He had spent an uncomfortable night alone in the barn, drifting in and out of sleep, and each sleep troubled by dreams, first of Tobias, then of Salvis, then of Carrik and Bellum and Luke. And Esram. Always there was Esram, threading his way through each dream like a snake, so like Luke in his appearance but a million miles apart in any other way. Petroc's ribs still hurt from where Esram had kicked him yesterday and, to make things even worse, the night had turned unexpectedly cold, so once he was awake, it had been difficult to get back to sleep.

As he slowly forced himself to wake up, he realised with a shock that it must be quite late. The sun was already streaming through the high open window of the barn. He yawned and sat up, wincing against the pain as his bruises made themselves known. It was still not very warm and he wrapped the blanket around himself like a cloak.

He was very hungry. The girls had left him the bottle and he drank deeply, then he picked two big apples from the tree, and the water and the apples were his breakfast; all the food he had. They did not satisfy his hunger, but they would have to do. He began to understand how Cherry must have felt with only fruit and water for food. At least in Bellum's castle they were able to eat the leftover scraps.

He went to the well and splashed cold water over his face to bathe the eye that was so sore.

The girls had not been happy to leave him there, especially Cherry, who had been sent to a strange home with someone she had only just met, but Petroc had been adamant. Something seemed to have happened to him when he called to the King, it was almost as if his old fighting spirit had returned.

He decided to inspect the farmhouse, and he paused briefly by Tobias' grave.

"Oh Father, I know this is what you would want," he whispered. "I know this will bring you peace in your spirit, just as it does to me."

The damage to the farmhouse was as bad as it could possibly be. The first thing they must do was replace the roof and front door, then shutters for the windows. But how? Where would they start? And what would they use? They would need wood and thatch and ropes and ladders, not to mention hammers and saws.

There was no longer an upstairs, as its floor had been completely destroyed by the fire. The bedroom where he had slept, by a window that looked out at the stars, had gone.

A sudden noise sent him to the doorway. Clattering across the yard was the oldest, most battered cart he had ever seen, and on it, in the middle of a huge pile of belongings, sat Martha and Delfi. The cart was being pulled by Amos who had harnessed himself to the shaft, and it was being pushed by Cherry and Morwen. They must have left home well before dawn.

Cherry waved. "Petroc! It's us! We're here!"

"I can see that," he grinned, and ran to meet them. "Here, let me take the back of the cart."

"We have pushed it all the way from the Bay of Dolphins so we can push it across the yard," she replied. "Besides, your ribs still hurt."

She was right there. Each breath Petroc took seemed to bring more pain.

"Where did you get it? We have no cart any more."

Delfi replied. "It belonged to my father, Josh," she said softly. "He will not need it, so we... we borrowed it."

There was an awkward silence at the mention of Josh, the traitor's, name. Josh had disappeared when Salvis died and none had seen him since, though many rumours were being spread around.

Morwen helped first Martha and then Delfi down from the cart and it was suddenly brought home to Petroc how old and frail his mother had grown. When had she become so old? Was it when he had been captured by Carrik or was it when Tobias was killed?

"Mother, you should sit down," he said, and went to help her, but she pushed him away.

"Boy, it would seem that you are the one needing help. Look at you! You can hardly walk! Who blackened your eye?"

"It is a long story," Petroc said ruefully, "and the one who did this came off worse... I think."

Martha had forgotten him. She was staring at what remained of their home.

"Oh, Petroc, what shall we do? We have no house left! Bellum has taken it all!"

For the first time Amos stepped forward and spoke to them. He had been finding his breath after the long, gruelling walk. The cart had been heavy and he was no longer a young man. Folk seemed to be growing old so quickly in these troubled times.

"Things are not so bad, sister," he said with a confidence that he did not feel. "The first thing we must do is to get a roof on, the rest may follow later."

"But how, Amos?" Martha cried, very close to tears. "Oh Amos, Amos, it is hopeless!"

Only Morwen was not dismayed. "Lord Veritan said that we should begin work and the King would send all the help we would need. That is what we should do."

Her brother laughed harshly. "Oh yes? And will Veritan chop the wood we need? And cut the reeds for thatch?"

"No," Morwen said quietly, "but it seems there are those who will." She pointed her hand across the field towards the Dark Forest. "See, there are people coming now from the farms."

They arrived in silence, a long line of those who had once been their neighbours and friends. Some carried timber, some rushes, flax and straw, some tools, others grain and food. Some even had money to give.

There was Raldi the carpenter; Martha had fed his children when he had no work. There was Simeon the boatman; Tobias had rescued his pet dog when it had fallen through the thin layer of ice over the river during the Time of Snows. And Mara, Morwen had befriended her daughter when she was learning to walk. And Daris, from the farm next to theirs; Petroc had helped him mend his fences after a storm.

Raldi was their leader and spoke for them all.

"We heard you had returned. Tobias was a good man and loyal to the King as we all are. We have come to repay your kindness to us. By tonight your house shall have its roof. Come friends, we shall set to work."

Morwen's heart leapt. "The King did not desert us!" she cried.

In the Royal Palace the King spoke to Salvis and to the Unseen Lord on the Third Throne.

"It is time! Now my people are ready to receive my Power!"

"It is time," Salvis agreed.

The assembled servants dropped to their knees and bowed their heads to the ground as the King and Salvis each raised their right hand, palms outward, towards the Unseen Lord on the Third Throne.

That Unseen Lord moved, and the Hall's silver light deepened to the colour of fire, and flames were sent from the thrones so that the marble floor turned red as blood. A mighty rush of wind travelled three times around the Hall. Then it was very still and quiet. The King and Salvis joined their hands and held them over the Third Throne. The Three were still One and the One was Three and yet power had been sent out from the Third Throne: a power that would be given to the people of Karensa to fight against the enemy and a power that could change each of their lives.

Petroc and Morwen stood with their backs resting against the new front door.

Morwen shook her head almost in disbelief. "Brother, it seems the impossible has come about. We have a roof, we have a door, we have shutters on the windows. We even have a table and benches made from the left over wood. Oh, the King has been so good to us!"

Petroc, too, had never expected them to accomplish so much in a day. But he was grateful to their friends.

"It was not the King! It was people returning our kindness!" he snapped. "It is them we should thank, Morwen, not the King."

"The King... the King..." Morwen struggled for the right words. "The King organised it," she said at last, and went to help Martha with the supper before he could shout her down.

They had brought plates, beakers and cooking pots from the cave house and Martha had cooked them a fine supper of meat and vegetables, crusty bread and sweet fruit pies that she had baked last night before she had gone to bed.

All of their friends were invited to stay. They sat around the long table and, as it grew dark, Martha lit the candles she had brought.

Petroc honoured Amos by giving him the place at the head of the table, which should have been his seat as the only son of Tobias and so head of the family.

Amos stood up before they began to eat.

"My friends, we thank you for your help," he said simply. "Martha's family now has a home, the home that belongs to them by right. Without your help we could not have done all this work. Eat now, eat your fill of what we have provided."

"One moment, brother," Martha pulled at his sleeve. "Before we begin, should we not remember Salvis? He was so good to us. He gave us hope when there was none. He healed us when we were sick. He encouraged us. Now he has given my family back their home."

"You are right," Raldi agreed. "When we all ran away he went to meet Bellum on his own."

"We must never forget him," Martha agreed.

Cherry said, "I saw him die. To the end he still cared for each one of us."

Petroc felt anger rising in the very pit of his stomach. He too had waited on Salvis to deliver them, all those months in Bellum's stronghold he had waited and trusted in Salvis, but Salvis would not fight to take back that which was his own.

Not wanting to upset Martha, Petroc slipped out quietly and went for a walk. When he had calmed down, he remembered that he was still hungry and that he needed his supper, so he went back to the farm, hoping to slip in without being noticed.

At once he knew that something had happened. Inside the farmhouse there was an air of excitement and laughter. There was a special atmostphere that he had never experienced before. It was like stepping into a warm bath.

"Oh, Petroc," Morwen cried. "Petroc, Salvis has been here! We did not see him but he has given us his power!"

"It was like a fire," Cherry exclaimed. "His power came to each of us like a fire!"

Raldi and his friends seemed to have gone completely mad. They were dancing and singing in strange new words that Petroc had never heard before, as though they had drunk too much wine. Yet there had been no wine with the meal.

Even Martha was changed. The years seemed to have melted away and once more she was the mother Petroc remembered. "My son, it is true! The King has given us his own power. It is here, in our hearts!"

She threw her arms around him so that he cried out in pain, for his ribs were still very sore. Then, she did an amazing thing. She put her hands on the very place where it hurt and a sensation like pins and needles travelled through his body.

"Salvis would not want you to be hurt," she said simply.

He pulled away.

"You are imagining things, all of you! Salvis is not here. You just wish he was, that is all. Salvis is dead."

"Oh, Petroc," Morwen said, "you know he is alive. You saw him yourself on the beach."

"It was a ghost," he argued. "Look, when I can touch him, when I see him eating and drinking with us, then I shall believe he is alive. Not until then."

The strange thing was, his ribs no longer hurt.

Chapter 9

Ploughing and Planting

The days became weeks and the weeks months and soon the Time of Plenty became the Time of Gathering. Now the hedgerows on the island of Karensa were bright with berries and the mornings were misty and cool.

Now the farm looked more like the home where Petroc and Morwen had grown up. Although the house was still without a first floor, Morwen and Cherry had made partitions out of sheets that Martha had brought with her from the cave house. Amos and Petroc had a bedroom in one far corner of the large room and Martha and the girls slept in another corner.

Martha had rugs for the floor to keep them warm when the Time of Snows arrived. Amos had rebuilt the tiny wash-house and there was always a fire with hot water to wash themselves and their clothes.

In the fields, Amos and Petroc, Morwen and Cherry had worked hard from dawn to dusk. Fences were repaired and walls rebuilt with dry stones. With two old ploughs, given to them by Raldi the carpenter, the four of them had managed to plough two of the three fields they owned. They would leave the third field fallow until next year. It was back-breaking work. They had no horses or oxen, so the ploughs had to be pulled by hand, each taking turns to be harnessed. By the time both fields were done, the girls, especially, felt there was not a muscle or bone in their bodies that did not hurt.

Still, it was done! Petroc had grown strong again. The hard work had built up his muscles and Martha's cooking had filled him out so that he was no longer weak and spindly. Only Cherry seemed to suffer. Her foot now seemed even more lame, although she would never complain, even when the others could tell that it hurt.

With the money their friends had given them on the day the roof was built, they had bought chickens for the yard so they had a supply of fresh brown eggs. They also bought a few sheep that would give them fine lambs before the Time of New Birth next year. They had a goat, so there was milk every day. They still had enough money to buy seed, and then still some left.

Each evening, as they sat down for supper, they would speak of all the good things that the King and Salvis had brought into their lives, for they were sure that this was all due to the King's blessing. Had he not sent Lord Veritan to tell them what to do? He had promised them they would have all they needed, and they did, and still more.

One day in seven, the friends who had helped them would come to the farmhouse, bringing their families, and they would speak of the King and of Salvis his son. Sometimes, Delfi would sing while Cherry played her lyre. Cherry was very musical. She would even make up songs for Delfi to sing, songs about Salvis. Others soon joined them until the farmhouse was full.

People were changed. They seemed to have a new strength within. They had no fear of each other, just as there had been no fear on the island before the war. As new people joined, they too received the King's power. Sometimes they would sing in a wonderful new language they had been given: a special language with words of ancient days. This seemed to give them even more power and energy.

Only Petroc did not change. He still waited to see Salvis with his own eyes and touch him with his own hands before he believed.

Today they were blackberrying, Petroc and Morwen, Cherry and Delfi. They had walked to the cliffs overlooking Black Rock Bay, where the brambles grew thick and were heavy with fruit. Now their baskets were full and their mouths stained purple with the berries they had eaten.

Cherry laughed at Delfi.

"You have eaten more than you have gathered," she exclaimed.

"My basket is full," the little girl protested. "I have as many as any of you."

More than any of them, Delfi had been changed by the King's power. She had a new boldness. She was no longer shy or afraid, nor yet bowed down by what her father Josh had done in betraying Salvis, although she was still ashamed.

Morwen, always the practical one, sighed deeply. "We should go home. Mother will want us to get the fruit washed and preserved... Petroc, why do you laugh?"

"Home," he replied, "the farm really is our home again. It was worth all our hard work. Father would be so proud of us!"

His remark was greeted by silence. Finally Morwen said, "We all worked hard, but the King blessed us. He sent us good friends to help, and he has made our money last so that we could buy everything we needed. And he sent Uncle Amos to us. We should never have been able to do all this on our own."

Petroc frowned. "I don't seek a quarrel, you must have your opinion, but I shall have mine... Let's just rest here for a while. Do you remember the time Luke and I went down to Black Rock Bay, and Father caught us? He was so angry!"

"He had forbidden you to go there," Morwen pointed out. "He said it was dangerous."

"It's not so bad! It was great, leaping from one rock to the next."

"Would it have been so great if you had fallen into the sea?" Morwen replied, her voice rising.

"Look!" Delfi cut across their argument. "Look, the dolphins are playing again!"

They watched as the dolphins leapt and dived through the surf, their grey bodies glistening silver in the sun.

Suddenly Cherry asked, "What has happened to Bellum? He seems quiet. Do you think he has decided to stay in his castle and leave us alone?"

"Not him," Petroc replied. "He'll be planning something. We should be prepared."

"I did see Esram and Carrik," Morwen told them, "when I went to the village with Mother. Carrik looks just ordinary now. He doesn't wear that serpent thing on his tunic. He spoke to us. He said hello. He just seemed like anyone else, really. I was not afraid of him, or Esram either."

A chill crept down Petroc's spine bringing with it a sense of dread that he could not explain. It was not fear. It was more a feeling that something was coming that he had no power to stop.

"Let's go home," he said abruptly, pulling Cherry to her feet. "We have to get the fruit prepared."

Amos was splitting logs in the yard just like Tobias used to do. It seemed a lifetime ago. When he saw them coming, he stopped, almost as though he had been waiting for them.

"You do have a mighty lot of fruit there! Martha will be pleased with you."

"I've worked hard," Delfi said, holding up her basket for inspection. It was full, but it was smaller than the others, yet no one told her so.

"You've done well, child," Amos said. "Now go and show Martha. You will need to get those cleaned before supper time because important decisions have to be made today."

He would say no more, even though Petroc glared at him. In Petroc's eyes the farm belonged to Martha, Morwen and himself and as the only man he felt any decisions should be made by him.

It was no use pressing Amos or even Martha. When she was asked she simply said, "First things first. The fruit will go bad if it is left. We shall see to that first. When that is preserved we shall have supper and then we shall talk."

So they set to work, and soon they had a shelf full of pots of jelly and jam ready for the long, cold months of the season called the Time of Snows.

At last, when supper was eaten, Amos and Martha seemed ready to talk.

Amos was the one who spoke. "It is time I returned to my own farm," he said gently. "I must see how my sons have fared on their own and whether our crops are sown. I have asked Raldi to keep an eye on you all, but in any case I shall return in a few days. Meanwhile, Petroc, I feel you and Morwen should be able to plant the seed. The hard work, the ploughing, is done. You must have helped Tobias many times?"

"Yes, we have," Petroc said slowly, "but Uncle, I feel there is more?"

"Yes, there is," said Amos. He took a deep breath. "I feel Martha should come with me, and Delfi too, and that they should stay there on the far side of the island."

Morwen gasped. "Mother! You cannot leave!"

"Your mother will be more comfortable there during the hard season," Amos explained. "She should not be sleeping on the floor! Delfi, the people on the far side of the island will not know who you are. They will not know you are Josh's daughter. Oh, yes, I have seen the way they look at you and the way they speak to you in the village. It will be a kinder life for you there."

"I do not care!" Delfi protested. "I want to stay here. This is my family now!"

"My family shall be yours," Amos told her. "You will still have Martha to care for you. Delfi, it is for the best. Then, when the Time of Snows is over we shall review the situation. We shall return when the time is right."

A tear rolled down Cherry's cheek.

"Oh Martha, you have been a mother to me since I have been here! Please do not go!"

"I have to," Martha said, very close to tears herself. "I found the time in the cave house so hard. The damp got through to my bones. The farmhouse will still be cold, although it is not damp. Amos is right. I cannot bear the hardship any more."

"We will get you a bed," Cherry cried desperately. "We will ask Raldi to make you one!"

"It is not just that. If it were, that would be easy to solve. I... I have not been well lately, children. When the King sent the new power, it rolled back the years and it is true that I do feel stronger, but the Time of Snows is coming and the King expects us to be wise. Now, I need someone to care for me as in the past I have cared for you."

"We will!" Cherry told her. "We will take it in turns!"

It was Petroc who settled things. He knew the right thing to do and he was brave enough to face the truth.

He put a protective arm around Cherry's shoulders.

"They must go," he said simply.

Morwen, watching silently, grew uneasy. Seeing Petroc and Cherry together made her feel left out of their lives. It was as though they had a secret part of themselves that no one else knew about.

Morwen was jealous.

Chapter 10

The Feathered Thieves

The departure next morning was very subdued.

It was with heavy hearts that Petroc, Morwen and Cherry watched as the old cart rumbled off across the meadow to make the long journey to the far side of the island.

Only once, Delfi looked back and waved, and then they were gone.

"Well," Morwen said sadly, "Now we really are on our own, at least until Uncle Amos returns. Petroc, it seems you must take on his responsibilities. Where do we start?"

"We start," Petroc replied, "by deciding who is to do what. When that is done, then we must lose no time in planting that seed. We can never be sure when the first snows will fall and then it will be too late."

He was so ready with his answer that it was plain that he must have been giving it some thought. Actually, he had lain awake into the early hours of morning, turning things over in his mind. He did not want his mother to leave, but he admitted that she was not looking well and it was the best way. He was also determined that the farm would continue to prosper while Amos was away.

"Morwen is the best cook," Cherry said quickly. "She should take Martha's place."

Morwen was not happy with that. "You were last here! You have spent your life being a lady's maid! I know the work on the farm. I should be the one to help Petroc in the fields. And you have a bad leg or foot or whatever it is. That will slow you down."

"It will not!" Cherry cried. "When has my lameness ever kept me from playing my part? I have worked as hard as you and more!"

Petroc, realising that he had to stop a full battle raging, placed a restraining hand on each of their shoulders.

"You shall take turns to cook and clean the house. One day Morwen, the next Cherry."

"What about you?" Morwen was too angry to listen to reason.

Petroc shrugged. "If you think I would be more use cooking than out in the fields, then I must take my turn."

"No... no of course not," Morwen muttered. "You are bigger and stronger than either of us. You should work on the farm as our father did. And today I shall cook and I shall milk the goat and I shall feed the hens."

"Today we plant seed," Petroc said firmly. "All of us. We can feed the hens first and milk the goat, but then we must all help to sow the seed. We have three bags of seed. That is one each. The three of us should get it done in a day."

"What about supper?" Morwen asked indignantly. She was not at all sure she liked being told what to do by her brother, who was only a year older than herself.

"We have cold meat and fruit and bread. That

will do for today. Now, the sooner we start, the sooner we shall be done. Morwen, you should do something with your hair."

Morwen gasped. Her mouth dropped open. Lately she had taken to wearing her thick hair loose so that it fell down her back in red-gold waves, but now she thought that Petroc had gone too far.

"You shall not tell me how to do my hair!" she cried.

"Morwen, as it is you will spend all day pushing it out of your eyes. It will take precious time."

"It would be better to braid it," Cherry agreed. "I'll do it for you, if you like?"

"I can do my own hair, thank you!" Morwen retorted, her face red and warm tears of humiliation pricking her eyes. "You feed the hens!"

She thought it was unfair of Petroc to tell her what to do and even more unfair of Cherry to take his side.

One day, she thought, I shall prove to both of them that they do not know everything there is to know. One day soon.

Sowing the seeds was the part of farming Petroc liked the most. It was the reward for the back-breaking work of clearing the fields and ploughing.

By this time next year they would have a fine crop of their own to harvest.

They took a field at a time, dividing it into three. That way they could work together and encourage one another. Before long they were laughing as they each tried to finish their section first.

By mid-afternoon the job was done.

"These crops will grow strong," Morwen said as she surveyed the land. "I believe the King will bless our hard work."

Petroc's face darkened. "Our hard work will make the crops grow, not the King. Come on, I'm hungry, even if you two are not. Let's go home."

As they crossed the last field Cherry stopped and pointed to the sky. She gave a cry of fear.

"Look! Look! Birds! Crows! Hundreds of them!"

"Oh no," Morwen gasped. "They are going to eat the seeds!"

They stood like three statues frozen in time as the army of black feathered thieves descended on their fields. Within minutes they had stripped them of every single seed.

The girls were clinging together. Cherry was crying.

"What shall we do?" Morwen said desperately. "I have never seen the birds do that, never before. What made them do it, Petroc? Such things never happened when our father was alive."

As she spoke a picture of Lord Bellum flashed across Petroc's mind. Without words he knew that Lord Bellum was responsible. He also knew that Carrik, no matter how friendly he might seem, had been furious that the King had given them the farm. Petroc's response was to stride off in the opposite direction and walk away.

He never knew why his steps took him to Black Rock Bay. Maybe it was because he was thinking yesterday of how he and Luke had gone there together?

He scrambled down the steep cliff path. He knew that this bay was the most treacherous on this part of Karensa, but he welcomed the danger. He wanted to forget all caution. How could he have been so stupid as to think that Carrik would simply let them take control of their farm? If the King was as powerful as Morwen and the others said, why did he let Bellum send the birds?

He pushed away the thought that he, himself, had refused to give any credit to the King for the way the farm had grown.

He stood on a black shiny rock near the sea's edge. It was as close to the foaming water as he could get. He wanted danger. He wanted to take risks.

"Why?" he shouted at the sea, "Why did you go back home, Luke? Why didn't you stay here with us?"

Then he shouted at the sky.

"Salvis, if you can hear me, do something! Don't just give up and die like you did before! Help me! What am I going to do? We have no more seed! Even if we were to sow more seed, the birds would only eat it again!"

Then he began to leap from rock to rock, defying nature.

"Bellum, you won't bring me down!" he yelled at the top of his voice. "You tried enough times when I was your prisoner but you never did it, and you won't do it now!"

Suddenly, he realised that he was standing on a rock surrounded by water. The tide must have turned. It was what Tobias had warned him about so long ago. There was no safe way back to the shore. He would have to leap blindly and hope he landed on a rock, remembering where he thought they were.

Taking hold of his courage, he leapt into the air and landed safely. Then again, only this time his foot slipped and with a cry he fell into the sea.

He began to swim, but the current carried him not to the shore, but to the sharp rocks at the bottom of the cliff. The water was over his head and in his eyes. He struggled to the surface and took a deep gulp of air before the sea took him under again.

This time, as he surfaced someone took his hand. Through the spray he saw a face surrounded by fair hair.

"Luke?" he gasped. "Luke, is that really you?"

The hand was pulling him towards the shore until at last he lay face down on the shingle.

He forced his eyes to open.

It was not Luke.

It was Esram who had pulled him from the sea.

Coughing and spluttering, Petroc pulled himself to his hands and knees. He felt very sick.

"Esram! You! What are you doing here?" he spluttered and then he turned away and he really was sick.

Afterwards he felt much better.

He stared up at Esram who was as wet as he was. It was clear that he had risked his own life to save Petroc.

"Why did you do it? You hate me. Your uncle wants our farm. Why didn't you let me drown?"

The other boy gave him a strange look that was hard to understand. If Petroc had not known better, he might have thought that Esram wanted to be friends.

"I do not hate you," Esram said flatly.

"Well, Carrik does! And you did not treat me well when I was in Bellum's stronghold."

"That was then. Things have changed."

Petroc gave a short laugh. "Oh yes, things have changed. You have no power over me any more."

Esram shrugged. "We should return home. We both need to change our clothes and get dry and warm."

He pulled himself to his feet and headed back up the cliff where his pony stood waiting, leaving Petroc not only feeling weak, but confused.

Chapter 11

Go Forward

For what seemed like a long time, Petroc sat on the grassy cliffs and stared down at the water crashing on the rocks below, the silver spray hissing as the sea thundered nearer and nearer.

If Esram had not arrived, he could so easily have been down there now, washed in like driftwood with the tide. Each time he thought of it, he shuddered.

He had hoped that his clothes would dry out in the sun so that Morwen and Cherry would not have to know what had happened, least of all that he had been rescued by Esram, but they were now too many weeks into the Time of Gathering and the sun had lost its full power.

Far out on the rocks, by the headland, he could hear seals barking as they played in the wild spray. In the old days each creature had lived in harmony, side by side with man. That was why they had not been ready for the crows to attack and eat their corn. It would not have happened before.

Petroc thought longingly of those days.

"Salvis, you came to fight for the King, why did you let Bellum kill you?" he said out loud. Then, for a second his pride crumbled. "Salvis!" he shouted out to the sea, "If you really are alive, then help us! Help me! What can we do? We have no seed!

Next year we shall have nothing to harvest!"

Some of the seals had come closer and they were sunning themselves on the rocks near the shoreline. They were barking loudly. For a few brief moments, Petroc felt as though he was at one with them again. They seemed to be telling him to go back to the farm.

Petroc did a little dance of victory, right there on the cliff. The day's lost work did not seem to matter any more. There was only one way to go and that was forward. It was useless to look back to what was past.

He stood in the doorway of the farmhouse.

"You seem wet," Morwen observed, looking her brother up and down.

Petroc grinned. "I am wet. I fell into the sea. And what do you think? I met some seals at Black Rock Bay."

"Black Rock Bay?" Morwen's face turned red with anger. "You went to Black Rock Bay again? You know how dangerous it is. You deserved to drown!"

Petroc continued to grin down at her.

"Don't laugh!" Morwen shouted. "How shall I dry your clothes? You are wet through and through. Oh, Petroc, how could you?"

"But it was like the old days when we lived in peace with the animals. It was like that with the seals!"

His sister was not impressed. "So what? It is more important to get you dry than to stand here talking about seals. Cherry, what are you doing?"

Cherry was rummaging through the old wooden chest that stood by the window. She pulled out three bundles of cloth. The grey one she gave to Petroc. A soft olive green for Morwen. A dark wine-coloured one for herself.

"What are these?" Morwen still sounded cross.

"They are gifts for us. Your mother gave them to me before she left. She said we were to use them when they were needed. Well, Petroc is wet. And you and I are hot and dirty. We need them now."

The bundles turned out to be three new sets of clothes, a tunic and trousers for each of them. Martha must have worked deep into the night to get them finished before she left for the far side of the island.

They decided to try them on and were soon admiring each other; Petroc in grey, just like Salvis had worn when he was with them, Morwen in soft green that brought out the red in her hair and the green in her eyes and Cherry in deepest red that showed off her dark eyes and rosy cheeks.

Cherry burst into tears. Not a few tears trickling down her cheek, but floods of tears as though her heart would break.

"Cherry, what is it?" Petroc asked, watching her helplessly. "Is the colour not right?"

"Of course not!" Cherry sobbed. "Of course it is not the colour. It is just... just... your mother is so kind. She has treated me as one of her own."

"Yes," Morwen said quietly, "she would," and she went behind the curtain to be alone in her sleeping space. She began to cry too. Then she saw Martha's empty mattress and cried even more. Like Petroc, she too longed for the old days to return, but she knew that they had gone for ever.

When she was empty of tears, she went back and joined the others at the table and ate what supper she could. She was ravenously hungry, yet at the same time she found it difficult to take an interest in her food. It was only after they had all finished that Petroc voiced the thought that was on all their minds.

"So what shall we do?"

"I have looked into the purse. We still have enough money to replace the seeds," Morwen said. "I cannot think how it has lasted so long, but it has."

Cherry frowned. "But what is there to stop Bellum sending more birds and the same thing happening again?"

"Do you think Bellum did send them?" asked Morwen, sounding surprised.

"Yes!" chorused Petroc and Cherry.

Petroc went on, "Carrik hates us having the farm, no matter what he says. He has probably been watching everything we have been doing. He could easily have asked Bellum to send the birds. Bellum used to be a Lord of the Palace, just like Veritan. He would have that power."

"But..." Morwen chewed her lip thoughtfully, "But Carrik has been friendly."

"He is not as he seems," Petroc told her. "Just because Esram pulled me out of the sea, that does not make him my friend!"

At once he could have bitten off his tongue.

"Esram!" Cherry exclaimed. "Carrik's nephew, Esram? Esram pulled you out of the sea?"

Morwen was suspicious. "Why didn't you say?"

"This does not get us anywhere," Petroc tried to change the subject. "Sister, I do not know what you must be thinking of. You know well that Carrik and Bellum are our enemies. Did they not kill our own father? You should be thinking more of a plan to help us. What shall we do? We must decide."

Suddenly, as though she had been thinking about something for a while, Cherry got up from the table and went outside into the growing dusk. When she returned she was carrying two long sticks from the wood pile. Then, with a length of twine, she tied them together to form a cross. As Petroc and Morwen watched open-mouthed, she dressed the cross in her old clothes. Finally, she took a turnip from the vegetable store and placed it on top of the cross, first piercing it with the long knife that Martha used for preparing food. As a finishing touch, she crammed a woollen hat over it.

"There!" she said triumphantly. "To a crow it will look like one of us and when the wind blows it will flap the clothes, so that the birds will be too scared to come on the field."

First of all the others laughed, then they stopped.

"It might just work..." said Morwen.

Petroc grinned. "We could call it Lord Crow Scarer!"

"Lord Scarecrow," Cherry giggled. "That is his name. Lord Scarecrow of High Field!"

Petroc laughed with her, but Morwen scowled. She felt left out again; no matter how hard she tried to push the thought from her mind, it returned to haunt her like a soft voice whispering in her ear, "They do not want you any more."

* * *

Before they went to bed they made two more scare-crows and decided that first thing next morning they would all go into the village to replace the lost seed. They needed three bags, and that would be one each to carry. They would lock and bolt the farm, and trust that it would be safe until they returned. Then, they would have time to get the corn planted before Amos returned. Better than telling him there was nothing actually in his ploughed fields.

As Petroc brought in fresh logs for the fire, Morwen and Cherry washed the dishes. Cherry sensed that her friend was unhappy. She thought it was because she did not like their plans.

"I feel it is what the King would want us to do," she said, trying to reassure her.

"Maybe." Morwen turned to put away the plat-ters and, by accident, she kicked Cherry's bad foot. She was instantly sorry. Morwen was too soft-hearted to want to hurt anyone, no matter how she might feel.

"It will be fine," Cherry gasped, holding the foot in both hands.

"Oh, but I can see it hurts! Cherry... maybe if we went to the King's Palace he could make your foot better?"

"But I have always been lame."

"That is no reason to stay lame. I saw Salvis make sick people well many times while we were all living in the Bay of Dolphins. Once, he made Delfi well."

Cherry was still holding the sore foot.

"Let's sit by the fire. Tell me stories of Salvis."

"You've heard most of them."

"I love to hear them, again and again."

For a short while, Cherry had made Morwen feel better, but as they settled down in front of the blazing logs it was Petroc that Cherry snuggled up against, so that Morwen was left on her own.

Again the voice in her ear whispered that she did not belong any more.

Chapter 12

Only to Look

"Just look at the village!" Morwen exclaimed. "I have never seen the village like this before!"

It seemed as though the entire village was having a party, for it was teeming with people, and even on a day like this, with a grey sky and black clouds that threatened rain, the village square was bright with colour.

As well as the usual fisher-people's stalls selling herrings and mackerel, lobsters and crabs, there were many other stalls arranged around the cobbled square. Every trader was shouting his wares at the top of his voice, each trying to outdo the other.

"Sweet honey from my own hives!"

"Wool cloth in new colours!"

"Apples and quinces, pears and plums! All from my own orchards! All ripe and ready to eat!"

"Ribbons! Come ladies, bright lace and ribbons!"

Morwen stared longingly at the array of ribbons on this stall. Green ribbons would set off her new clothes and her red hair. Her hand reached up and touched her own plaits that had no decoration at all. Martha had always kept her well-supplied with hair ribbons back at the farm, but now she had none at all.

Petroc guessed her thoughts. There was nothing

his sister liked more than to comb and dress hair, her own or other people's.

"If we have enough money left over when we have bought our seed, then you shall both have new ribbons," he promised.

Ruefully Cherry ran her fingers through her short, black curls.

"I shall not need ribbons," she said sadly.

"You will," Morwen told her. "Your hair is beginning to grow, and besides, I have an idea what we could do with it. Oh, look over there! That man is swallowing fire!"

They stood at the back of the crowd and watched the fire eater.

"How does he not get burnt?" Morwen wondered.

Cherry smiled. "It is a trick. In Bellum's castle, he would often do this."

"You mean he is Bellum's man?"

"He was," Cherry said slowly. "Perhaps he has changed? See, he has ended now and there is the juggler. He was there, too, in the castle."

The juggler was followed by acrobats and before they had finished, the children moved away, because they had no money to put in the hat that was about to come round.

There were other things to see. There was dancing, men with maids, and side shows where, for a penny, you could try to knock some skittles down to win a prize.

"Oh, I wish it could always be so," Morwen sighed. "Why is there so much work and so little enjoyment?"

Petroc and Cherry did not reply. The truth was,

they were both thinking the same. Such pleasures, music and entertainment, could make you forget your problems.

In the centre of the market square a large crowd was gathering, and the girls clamoured to see what was going on.

Petroc's cry that they had work to do fell on deaf ears.

"It is Carrik!" Cherry gasped. "But he is so changed!"

"And those are Lord Bellum's men," said Morwen. "And they too are changed. They no longer look like his followers, do they? What has happened to them all? It must be that Bellum has decided not to be wicked any more?"

Petroc and Cherry could not believe that this was true, but they could not deny that Bellum's household was different now. They no longer wore their uniforms of black tabards with the coiled scarlet serpents, the emblem that Bellum had made his own. They were dressed in bright tunics of green, red and gold. They were no longer armed. Not one of them appeared to carry a sword. But it was more than that. They no longer appeared threatening; instead they seemed happy and relaxed and set for an enjoyable day out.

Petroc was uneasy. Terrible memories of Bellum's awful capabilities were still fresh in his mind.

"It is not so," he muttered. "It cannot be so..."

"Oh, Petroc, you are too suspicious! Let us at least hear what Carrik has to say."

Carrik was standing on a raised platform reading from a scroll. He was dressed in a simple russet tunic and like the other servants of Bellum's household, he carried no sword.

His voice, too, was not quite the same. It held no threat any more.

"Good people you have worked hard and lost much!" he cried. "The war is now over and we must forget our battles and live in peace. To celebrate, and as a token of his good intent, the Lord Bellum invites each of you to a feast in his castle. See, he even provides you with transport to take you there!"

He held up his hand and a cart rumbled across the village square. And what a cart! It was pulled by two horses of purest white and decorated with flowers of every colour. If it should rain, the cart had a roof of what seemed to be gold. The wheels were also gold while the shafts were made of silver. All four corners of the cart were decorated with multi-coloured ribbons of silk and satin.

"Oh, look, look!" Morwen laughed excitedly, "Everyone is getting in!"

This was not quite true. Many were getting on the cart, but many more were doubtful and were turning away.

"There are no guards on the gates of my master's castle," Carrik encouraged them. "It is not like the King's Palace. My master's house is open to any who choose to enter. Come, good people, forget your cares, forget your work for today. Have a holiday! Lord Bellum has a great banquet prepared!"

Morwen clapped her hands. "Brother, we must go!"

Petroc and Cherry stared at her as if they could not believe what she was saying.

"How can you?" Petroc cried. "How can you even think of it after all we have told you?"

"Morwen, it is not as it would seem," Cherry added. "We know what Bellum is really like. We have been prisoners in his castle!"

As she watched them standing so close together, Morwen felt something snap inside her. She was tired of them thinking that they knew more than she did. She was tired of being made to feel left out of their lives.

"That was before," she argued. "You can see that they are not the same. It cannot be so bad or the butterflies would not have gone there!"

"Butterflies?" Cherry asked bewilderedly.

"We did see some going there," Petroc explained. "But Morwen, you cannot follow a crowd of butterflies!"

Morwen stamped her foot in frustration and temper.

"Yes I can," she said stubbornly. "You keep telling me how you have both been inside Lord Bellum's castle and now I want to see for myself." As she saw their dismayed faces, she relented a little. "Look, I will not actually go inside. I just want to look through the gates, that is all. I promise. I know what I am doing! You should not worry about me. I can look after myself."

Before they could stop her she had pushed to the front of the crowd and climbed into the cart.

Petroc tried his best to follow, but by now the press of people was so great that he was pushed back, and the last he saw of his sister was the wave of her hand as, followed by many others who could not find room in the cart, the procession left the market square.

Petroc and Cherry stared helplessly at each other.

"What shall we do?" Cherry whispered. "Petroc, I feel I am to blame. If I had not joined your family, she would not have left left out."

Petroc scowled by way of an answer.

"Should we go after her?" Cherry added.

"We should get the seed for the farm."

"But Morwen..."

"Morwen made her choice. We have come here to buy seed. If we do not sow our crops very soon the first snows will be here and then we shall be in trouble next year when we have no corn to harvest. And make no mistake, Cherry, I am determined that I will restore my father's farm. It is what he would want, and it is what I want to do."

"But Morwen..."

"Morwen is my sister and she is in danger, I know that. If she is not back by nightfall I shall go after her."

"You would dare to enter that castle again?"

"Yes... if she is not back... but Morwen is not that foolish, Cherry. I do not believe that she will really go to Bellum... Now here is the corn merchant, so let us concern ourselves with the job which we came to do."

However, buying the corn was not so easy. Amos had been able to strike a deal with the corn merchant so that they paid a reasonable price, but the man was not so willing to bargain with two children. In the end they could only afford two bags of seed, not three.

"Oh, well," Petroc sighed, "One each to carry

equals one for each field."

"But Morwen..." Cherry said for the third time. "Oh, Petroc! I am really scared for her."

"Yes," said Petroc grimly. "So am I!"

Chapter 13

A Sea-green Butterfly

The procession wound its way slowly, briefly skirting the Dark Forest, and then across the Meadow of Flowers, towards Bellum's castle.

It was led by a group of musicians all dressed in tunics and trousers of bright colours, some with pipes, others with trumpets, some with cymbals, and others with drums, harps or lyres.

The people sitting in the cart clapped in time to the music, while others, walking behind, turned their steps into a dance.

Morwen sat at the back of the cart next to a man and woman with three not very well-behaved children; two boys who were squabbling, and a girl who was even worse, so Morwen's attention was divided between the musicians and listening to this family's conversation.

There was hardly time to think about the foolhardy thing she was doing, but even if she had time it would probably have made no difference. She was hurt, she was angry and she was tired of being poor. She was also curious to find out what the castle was really like inside.

It seemed that the mother of the family did not really want to go and was raising all sorts of objections. She had heard bad things about Lord Bellum. The father did not agree.

"It is all only gossip, and the children are looking forward to this. We cannot change our minds. It is too late."

"It is too late," the words echoed in Morwen's mind. She pushed the thought away as quickly as she could.

The eldest boy rewarded his father's trust by smacking his sister with his toy flute. She burst into tears. The father slapped the culprit, but his hand missed and landed on the wrong boy, so all three children began to howl in unison.

Morwen thought it was sad. She remembered the happy home where she and Petroc had grown up with loving parents, and she was so thankful for her caring mother and father. However, she had to put her parents out of her mind for she knew, only too well, what they would say to her now.

How could they know about Petroc and Cherry making her feel left out? She set her mouth in a hard line. The farm was all Petroc cared about.

By now they had crossed the Meadow of Flowers and Bellum's castle towered above them, yet it did not seem to loom as darkly as before.

Just as Carrik had told them, there was no guard set on the gates, so they clattered across the wooden bridge into the courtyard. The castle now had a moat, and she shivered as she looked down on it from the cart because the waters appeared to be unusually black and cold.

The people looked around in wonder, and now Morwen had to remind herself that she had promised not to go right inside the castle. She would just peep inside the door to see what it was like and then she would slip away unseen.

To her horror, as the last of the followers danced through the gates, the iron portcullis dropped down behind them.

A chill of fear gripped Morwen's heart. She refused to own up to it. She told herself that Bellum had probably shut the gates because the castle would not have room for any more guests. Then she looked at the vastness of the building and knew this was not true. It was big enough to hold every person on Karensa, if they wanted to go there.

Maybe there were wolves around, then? Or bears? Whatever the reason, now that she was here, she may as well look around. She was not going to come all this way for nothing, and besides, she did not want to get home too early or she would not give Petroc and Cherry enough time to get really worried. She wanted them to worry.

They were in a square courtyard surrounded on all sides by walls of grey stone. In the centre of the courtyard stood a high platform. It must be here that Salvis had died? It seemed just an ordinary platform and today it was hung with silk banners of red and gold. Quickly, Morwen pushed a picture of Salvis' kind face from her mind.

Carrik climbed up the steps to the stage.

"Welcome, welcome to you all! Lord Bellum will greet you soon, but for now you must come, come inside. Tonight we have a great feast prepared. We have declared today to be a holiday for all!"

Eagerly they climbed down from the cart, each anxious to be the first inside this splendid place. Morwen let the quarrelling family go first, so she was the very last to get down. As she stepped from the cart, she lost her footing and stumbled, for the cart was very high and there was no one left to help her.

A hand took hers and she looked up to thank the kind person. She found herself staring into Lord Bellum's eyes.

Morwen pulled back in fear, but today Bellum was smiling, not his customary mocking sneer but a smile that seemed almost warm and caring. He seemed so changed. Gone was the armour and black silken clothes. Gone was the sword and shield. He was still finely dressed, but today he wore blue and silver, which were Lord Veritan's colours. He held her hand long after she had recovered her balance.

"Little Morwen, is it not?" he said softly. "You see, child, I was right. Did I not say that one day soon you would walk into my castle of your own free will?"

"I... I... I cannot stay," she stammered. "I promised my... my brother, I would be home..."

Bellum laughed. His laugh was filled with music.

"You know very well that Petroc is concerned only for Cherry," he whispered in her ear.

Morwen felt her colour rise in shame to think that even Lord Bellum knew how she was feeling.

In spite of all her fears, Morwen was curious, and almost like someone half-asleep she allowed herself to be led by Lord Bellum himself into the shadows of the very castle where she had promised not to go.

It was beautiful!

The scene took her breath away. As they passed

through the huge oak door they were in a great hall, bigger than Morwen could ever have imagined. This hall was pillared and vaulted and hung with drapes of all colours that reflected dimly in the black, marbled floor. Flowers and vines were wound round each pillar.

At one end of the hall, and down two sides, were tables already laden with food. In the centre part many people stood talking and laughing, all dressed in rich velvets and silks and furs. Morwen noticed that only the men wore tunics and trousers. The ladies were dressed in a fashion she had never seen before. They did not wear trousers, but strange gowns that reached to the floor. Their hair was dressed with circlets of sparkling jewels.

Morwen looked down at her own simple clothes and knew that the green wool seemed drab by comparison. She felt like a caterpillar in a room full of butterflies.

Bellum placed a jewelled finger beneath her chin and this time she did not shrink from him. He snapped his fingers and two servant girls came running and bowed low before him on their knees.

He motioned to them to rise. "You know what you have to do," he said. He did not use the same soft tones to them that he had used to Morwen. His voice now seemed harsh. "This maid is to sit at my table tonight. See that she is suitably attired. And see you do it well, or you will answer to me!"

The two girls scrambled to their feet and gestured to Morwen to follow them across the hall and up a flight of winding, stone stairs.

They led her round and round the winding steps until they reached a small turret room. For a brief moment Morwen was scared that they were going to lock her inside, all her old fears of Lord Bellum returning, but no, they came in with her and there was nothing to fear. It was a bedroom, at one end of which was a marbled bath of warm, scented water.

The taller of the girls pointed to the bath.

"Please?" she said. She seemed afraid. Morwen could not think why she would be afraid of her.

"You mean I must get in there?" she said, swallowing hard. Many times she had bathed in the ocean but she had never had a bath before.

"Yes. Take off your clothes. Come, mistress, you are safe. There are only ourselves here and no-one will enter. Please, do not be too long. Our master desires to see you at supper."

Morwen rather liked being called mistress. It made her forget she was poor, and it definitely made her forget that she was only twelve years old.

So she lay back in the warm bath and let the girls wash and perfume and later dry her long hair.

Afterwards she reached for her old clothes but the same girl pushed her hand away.

"They will not do at all, mistress," she said. From a wardrobe she took a gown of green silk. She slipped it over Morwen's head and laced it up, then she dressed her hair.

At last, after what seemed like an eternity, she motioned to the smaller girl, who brought out a full length mirror of polished glass.

Morwen's heart raced at the reflection she saw. The farm girl was gone. The child was gone. In her place was a fine maiden, even a princess, and yes, the rock pool had not lied that day on the beach.

Her face was fair indeed.

The caterpillar peasant child had gone and a lovely sea-green butterfly had emerged.

The gown felt strange, but it looked well on her and the colour was like nothing Morwen had ever seen, a sea-green silk shot with silver. The bodice had long, narrow sleeves and was laced tightly down to the high waist. From there the garment fell in graceful folds to her feet, which were clad, not in boots, but in soft, velvet slippers. Her hair was left loose, held only by a green ribbon.

Wonderingly, she held out the skirts of the gown in front of the mirror and found that with every movement they reflected a different shade, which made her think of all the moods of the ocean.

"Oh," she breathed. "Oh, it is so beautiful. I had never thought to wear anything so beautiful. Thank you so much."

"Do not thank us, thank Lord Bellum," the smaller girl told her. "And mistress... please, have a care..."

The taller girl flashed her companion a warning glance. "Lord Bellum has many such lovely things," she said. Just as she spoke, there was a tap on the door. "That will be your escort for the feast. Shall we let him in, mistress? And yes, you do look beautiful."

Morwen nodded her agreement, not knowing what to expect. She certainly did not expect it to be this tall, fair-haired youth, dressed from head to foot in cloth of silver.

"Esram!" gasped Morwen.

Chapter 14

Castle of Shadows

The admiration in Esram's eyes, as he stared down at her, made Morwen giggle nervously. Her new clothes felt strange, but another glance in the mirror reassured her that they did not look strange at all.

Esram held out his hand to her and she placed her own hand in his. She was surprised how soft and white his hands were, but then, he had never had to pull a plough or hoe a field. She was very aware that her own hands were brown and freckled and roughened by farm work.

He made no comment, but led the way down the stairs and back into the Great Hall.

They stood together in the doorway, taking in the scene that met their eyes. The hall was a blaze of colour and now, with evening falling, it was lit by many torches, their flames flickering and dancing and making the colours seem even brighter than they really were. The long table at the top of the hall and the other tables leading from it down the two sides, were all set with gold platters and goblets and each was piled high with food. There were jugglers and acrobats, the ones they had seen in the village square, and even now the guests were taking their seats at the tables.

Morwen pulled Esram to a seat near the door

where they would not be noticed, but Esram held her back.

"We are to sit at Lord Bellum's table tonight," he said. "It is our master's own command and it is well to obey him."

Morwen felt a small shiver of unease, but she pushed it away and followed Esram to their places at the high table, to the left of a massive throne-like chair. Carrik was sitting on a smaller chair to the right.

As they took their seats, there was a loud fanfare of trumpets, and at once everyone rose to their feet as Bellum and his entourage came into the hall.

Morwen's knees began to shake. If only she could have sat where no one could see her. Yet part of her was enjoying herself, the new clothes and the feeling of being grown up and important. Her heart began to thump with excitement and her eyes had a new sparkle. There was something exciting and dangerous about Bellum. Something she did not yet understand, but something which made her want to know more.

If he had seemed splendid before then he seemed even more so now.

He could not have found his crown, for his head was bare, but in spite of that he looked like a king.

This evening he was dressed from head to foot in black and gold. However, Bellum's gold had no real lustre; it was dull, almost like a false gold, as if it needed to be polished to make it shine.

Yet Lord Bellum was still magnificent and as he took his seat on his throne and indicated that all should be seated too, he smiled at Morwen and Esram. His teeth were very white and his eyes gleamed, sometimes black, sometimes amber in the torchlight.

"Little Morwen, so you stayed after all," he said softly.

Morwen met his gaze. The farm and Petroc and Cherry seemed a thousand miles away, and her new clothes had given her boldness. She was no longer so afraid.

"Yes, I am still here, my lord," she replied.

"That is well! That is very well. You make a fine couple, you and Lord Esram. He has a promising future in my household when he is grown. His uncle, Lord Carrik, has served me well."

Carrik, seated on the other side of him, saluted her. A small voice in her heart said, this man killed your father, but she deliberately chose not to listen.

Lord Bellum was still speaking. "You see, Morwen, I was right, you are passing fair, and when you are grown to a young woman you will grace my court with Esram." Morwen felt her face burn and Esram, too, looked embarrassed at his obvious meaning.

She had no time to dwell on it, for supper was being brought in, and she had never seen food like this in all her days. There was every meat and fish she could think of, fruit piled high on dishes of gold and some food she had never even seen before. There were many different kinds of bread and spicy sauces. A tempting variety of desserts too. And the wine was so plentiful that it flowed like water.

Morwen had never drunk wine before. She took a sip from her golden goblet. The red liquid was rich and sweet and so she drank some more.

She was horrified when a picture of her brother

and Cherry flashed into her mind. She remembered that once they had been prisoners here and made to eat scraps from the table at banquets like this. On such an occasion Bellum had told Petroc that their father had died, and had been so cruel in the telling...

As if he read her mind, Lord Bellum whispered, "Your brother could have had this too, my dear, if he had desired it," and she comforted herself that this, at least, was true.

All through the long banquet the musicians played for them, and all through the banquet Morwen sipped at the wine in her golden goblet. When they had finished eating, Carrik stood up and raised his goblet high.

"A health to Lord Bellum, the true ruler of Karensa!"

Morwen stood up with the others and was shocked as the room spun round.

"You have taken too much wine," Esram hissed in her ear. "Come, you must drink a toast to Lord Bellum. Hold on to my arm and raise your goblet." She stared at the wine in her hand. To be made into a fine lady and taken to a banquet was one thing; to deny the King was something quite different. "Oh, I cannot," she murmured, aware that many people were staring at her, including Lord Bellum himself who did not look pleased.

"You must," Esram whispered. "If you do not, Lord Bellum will be angry. Look, pretend."

He took the wine from her and held it to her lips. She tried not to drink it, but as he tipped the goblet, either she must drink it or she must let it spill on the table. She drank the wine. Lord Bellum appeared to be satisfied. Morwen felt terrible.

Carrik spoke again. "May we ask one more thing of you, Lord Bellum? Would you sing for us? None in all of Karensa has so great a gift in making music to touch the very soul."

Bellum smiled. He had obviously been waiting to be asked, and as the musicians played, he sang, soft and low, a haunting melody that made Morwen want to cry. She forgot that this man was her enemy and the enemy of the King and of Salvis. She forgot everything except the beautiful notes that filled her heart.

When the song was ended, even Bellum looked sad. With a shock, Morwen realised that there were tears in his eyes and, for a brief moment, she felt sorry for him.

"What is it, my Lord?"

"Ah, nothing, little Morwen, nothing," he said so quietly that only she could hear. "Except that with this very song I once ministered to the King..." His voice trailed away.

Curious again, she asked, "Then, why did you... why..."

"Why did I disobey the King?" Bellum smiled wryly. "Why indeed? But you see, little one, the King took away the worship that should have been mine."

"But... but he is the King!"

Without any warning, Bellum grew angry, and Morwen was afraid she had said too much.

"He is King for now, but not for ever. One day I shall..." Then he seemed to remember that this was a celebration. "Dancing!" he called. "We shall have dancing! The children must take the lead! I once promised little Morwen she should dance."

"I cannot! I cannot dance. I have never learnt!"

"Then I shall teach you," Esram said firmly. "It is easy. All you need to do is follow me," and as the music played, he took her hands and led her into the centre of the hall.

He was a good teacher, and soon she knew the steps and began to enjoy herself.

After a time she began to feel light-headed again.

"You should not have drunk so much," Esram said with unusual concern.

"I... I did not know it would do this to me..."

He led her away from the dancing. "Come, you need some fresh air, then you will feel better. Besides, I have something to show you."

The night air was cool to their cheeks and Morwen's head cleared as Esram led the way across the courtyard and then through another door.

She gasped with delight. "Oh, Esram, it is so lovely!"

"I knew you would like it," he said, and his eyes told her that he was trying desperately to please her.

"So this is where the butterflies came!" she breathed.

They were in a long, low room with many windows. The room was filled with green plants, palms and ferns and every other foliage that grew on the island of Karensa. The roof of the building was made of glass so that people might almost think they were not in a room at all. Amidst the greenery fluttered butterflies of every colour.

Morwen walked between the plants and as she did so, the butterflies' wings were like music to her. Just as before, she had never heard such a sad song, sadder even than the music Bellum had made.

She began to cry.

"What is it Morwen? You should not be sad. I thought you would like this place?" Esram sounded dismayed.

"It is the butterflies," she sobbed. "I know they want to be free."

Then she understood. She was no different from the butterflies. She was a prisoner like them in this place where even the gold had no shine.

Well, at least she could help them before it was too late. She ran to the nearest window and twisted the catch, opening it wide. Then the next window and the next.

"Butterflies, leave while you may!" she cried, and in spite of Esram's frantic attempts to stop her, the butterflies took their chance to escape. Soon all that was left in the room were the green plants.

"What have you done?" Esram gasped. "Oh Morwen, what have you done? What will Lord Bellum say? He was collecting those butterflies! He will not forgive you."

"I do not care!" she cried as the truth flooded into her heart. "I have been foolish! I will never serve Bellum! Never in a thousand years! This castle is not real! The King's castle is real! This is a copy, a castle of shadows!"

Her heart was thumping, and the room spinning as the wine and the moment overtook her and Esram caught her as she fell.

Chapter 15

Deny Your Fear

Petroc and Cherry walked home in silence. Petroc was too angry and afraid for his sister to say much at all, and Cherry's arms and back ached from carrying the heavy corn seed. Her foot hurt too. It had been more painful than ever since they had begun to restore the farm because she had very little time to rest. But it was not in her nature to complain. She was glad of a place to call home and if the work was hard, then she would endure it. She had become very close to Petroc, although she often thought about her former mistress, Zena, who had been so kind. Tas, Zena and Nolis were still all living in Bellum's castle and she knew that Zena was unhappy there.

Just like Petroc, she too was worried about Morwen. She had promised not to actually go inside Bellum's castle but that might not have been so easy when the time came.

Petroc's face was white. He felt as though he was in a battle. On one hand his sister was in danger and he should have gone after her and brought her back, but on the other hand his farm was in danger, too. They had to get the seed sown, if next year they were not to starve. He told himself again and again that this would have been his father's desire.

Privately Cherry thought that Tobias would have

put his daughter first, but she did not dare to say so.

When at last they rounded the last bend in the path and saw the farm and saw that Josh's old cart was standing outside the farmhouse door, Cherry uttered a cry of relief.

"Petroc, it is your uncle! It is Amos, come back already. We shall be safe now. He will know just what to do."

Petroc did not answer her. Morwen is not safe, he thought.

"Amos, Amos, we are so pleased you are home!" she called as they staggered in through the door and thankfully put down the two heavy bags they were carrying.

Amos replaced the lid on the cooking pot he had been stirring.

"So what is this?" he pointed to the corn seed. "Why was the seed not sown yesterday, as I asked? And why are there only two bags, not three? And where is Morwen?"

Suddenly, Petroc and Cherry both felt very tired. They had worked so hard, they had walked so far. They both felt as though they had failed, that in some way they had let Amos down.

As they sat on the hard wooden bench, Petroc told his uncle all that had happened while he had been away, with Cherry joining in with the occasional "yes" or "that's right."

When they had finished, Amos nodded thoughtfully. "I did feel in my spirit something was wrong. That is why I came back so early. Your mother and Delfi are both settled in their new home and my own land is being well-cared for by my sons, so I felt I should come back here."

"You are a good man, Uncle Amos," Petroc told him with a sudden rush of gratitude. "Without you, we should not have survived."

"Yes you would, Petroc," his uncle replied. "You are the son of Tobias and you will always survive. Do not ever forget it. Be proud of your father and of who you are."

Cherry asked, "What can we do?"

"Do?" The big man laughed. "Do? Why, we get the seed sown today, before it is too late, that is what we can do. Morwen will come home when she is ready. Do not forget that, just as Petroc is the son of Tobias, so Morwen is the daughter of Martha, my sister. She, too, will survive. Her loyalty to the King will carry her through. If she is not back by dark, then we must go after her. But first, we shall eat a meal. We are all hungry and not able to work without food."

"You do not realise the wickedness of Lord Bellum," said Petroc in a low voice. "Morwen might not be free to come home, even if she wants to."

"Then we shall fetch her!" Amos shouted at him. "But for now, boy, let us eat this meal!"

He began to fill their wooden dishes with stew. All at once the children realised how hungry they were and ate greedily.

As they finished there was a knock on the door.

Cherry went to answer it, but Amos pulled her back.

"No, let me go," he told her.

Petroc knew then that, in spite of his brave words, Amos was as uneasy as he was himself.

They need not have worried. Standing in the

doorway were Raldi, the carpenter, and Daris, the farmer.

"We sensed in our hearts that you were in trouble, and we have come to help," Raldi said simply. That again made Petroc uneasy. Since that first night when they said that the King had given them a new power, it was sometimes as though they knew each other's needs. Petroc had not been there. He had missed whatever it was that had happened.

"The King must have sent you," Amos replied, "For we are in need of your help." He told them the story. "If we all work hard, we should be finished by bed time. And this time our three new friends will help keep the crops safe." He pointed to the three scarecrows the children had made the day before. One was wearing Morwen's old clothes and it made Cherry want to cry.

"They are a good idea," Daris said. "I have been farming all my life and I never knew birds to steal the crops before. They have always been satisfied with berries from the hedgerows."

"They were sent by Lord Bellum, I know it," said Cherry. She turned to Petroc. "Oh Petroc, I feel Carrik still desires your farm. He will not stop until he gets it. Now he has Morwen under his control."

With everyone helping, the work was done much faster and it did not seem too long before the three scarecrows stood like guardians over the newly sown fields. As the old clothes caught in the breeze they flapped loudly, so the few birds that came to see what was going on, soon flew away, scared at what they did not understand.

Raldi and Daris went home and Amos left the

fields soon after, but Petroc and Cherry hung back, even though it was getting dark, a reminder that before long the Time of Snows would be here.

"We should go too," said Cherry. She was thinking of Morwen. What was she doing? How was she being treated? Cherry knew only too well that neither Bellum nor Carrik could be trusted, and neither could that trouble-maker Esram.

As they stood up, they saw a bright cloud coming towards them, its pastel colours reflecting the setting sun.

"Oh Petroc, it is the butterflies!" Cherry laughed, clapping her hands together in delight. "You told me about them. See how lovely they are!"

They stood perfectly still, for fear of crushing any of the gentle creatures as they flew all around them, just as they had flown around Petroc and Morwen on the day they had met Lord Veritan in the Meadow of Flowers.

Cherry laughed again. "Their wings sound like music! Wonderful music!" Her laughter died. "But it is a sad song! I believe they sing of danger and fear."

"They must have come from Bellum's castle. They must have seen Morwen."

"I know Morwen is not safe, Petroc! I know it! I feel it! Petroc, why did she go there?"

Petroc knew why. He had been feeling guilty all day. He knew that his sister was jealous of his friendship with Cherry.

"I shall go to Bellum's stronghold," he decided firmly, yet even as he spoke he felt a shiver of dread chill his very being. He was very afraid.

"Morwen is like a sister to me," Cherry told him.

112

"She was always a true friend. I shall come with you."

Petroc would have liked to refuse her help, but he was honest enough with himself to admit that he would need her support, even though she, too, would be afraid.

As the butterflies drifted away, she whispered in his ear, so soft that only he could understand.

"Petroc, we shall be together and we shall be brave. We shall help each other. It is time to overcome the past and to deny your fear."

Chapter 16

Who the Son Sets Free...

Morwen struggled to open her eyes. She was so cold. Her head hurt and as she sat up, she realised that she had no idea where she was or how she had got there.

The room was small and square, with a high window which barely let in enough light for her to see. There were bars at the window and the walls and floor were stone. The heavy door was locked and bolted.

It was a prison. Tears welled in her eyes and she did not try to hold them back, but let them pour down her cheeks. How could she have been so foolish? She had betrayed Petroc. She had betrayed her father, who had died for the King. She had betrayed Salvis. And worst of all she had betrayed the King himself by drinking the health of his enemy.

Of her own free will, she had walked into Bellum's stronghold. It had been easy. Her wounded pride, the fine clothes, the rich food and the admiration of others had all made it so easy. She knew that it would not be as easy to get out.

Trembling with cold and fear, she stood up and looked around. There was no escape. She might never see her family or the farm ever again. Bellum might have put her here to starve. There was not even a blanket, and the thin silk clothes she wore did not protect her from the damp stone walls. As her head cleared, she realised there were chains on her wrists, and with that discovery she dropped to her knees and began to cry as never before. Her body shook as she sobbed from her heart, calling first to Petroc, then to Tobias, then to Luke. None of these could help her.

At last she called to the person she had loved more than any; she called to Salvis, the King's son.

"Salvis, I am sorry, I am so sorry! I betrayed you! I was jealous of Cherry! I know I did wrong! Salvis, please forgive me, please help me!"

As she cried his name, her tears stopped, and just as he had on that first night at the farm, the King sent his power. It flowed through her like a waterfall of peace.

Morwen never knew how long she knelt there on the hard stone floor, just thinking about Salvis and all the wonderful things he did when they all lived at the Bay of Dolphins. That was how Esram found her when he unlocked the cell.

Esram held up his torch and the flames illuminated the cell with a flickering light.

What he saw left him speechless. He had expected to see Morwen broken and pleading to be set free, but instead her face was filled with radiant joy.

Puzzled, he stepped into the cell and shut the door behind him, resting the torch in an iron clamp on the wall. He knew there was something different in the room, something that he did not understand, something that he had never met before, but something that he desperately wanted for himself.

He knelt down beside her on the dirty floor. He knew now that he could never hurt her.

"Morwen," he said, with a new tenderness. "Morwen, do you know why I have come here?"

She turned her head towards him. Her eyes were brighter than any eyes he had ever seen.

"It must be to take me to Lord Bellum?"

Esram nodded. "He is very angry about the butterflies, Morwen. You know you will be punished, even... even worse?"

To his astonishment she smiled at him.

"Then I am ready," she said simply, knowing now that nothing mattered except that Salvis was her friend.

Esram was struggling. His heart was telling him that he needed to have this new thing for himself, but his mind was saying that if he did have it, he would lose all that seemed important to him. Suddenly she said, "Esram, you feel it too! You want the peace in your heart too."

"The King will not want me! I've done terrible things!"

"Yes, yes he would! As long as you're really sorry and tell him so, the King will forgive you and give you a fresh start!"

Esram looked at her. She had nothing. She was a prisoner in chains. Yet she had everything in the world.

All at once, his resolve crumbled, and there, on the damp, cold floor of the cell he gave his life over to the King and, for the first time ever, he knew the peace of the King's love and power in his heart.

"I have never felt like this before!" he gasped. "It... it's wonderful, it's the most wonderful thing..."

Morwen seemed even happier than he was. "We must go," she said. "Lord Bellum will be waiting."

"I cannot take you there now! I can no longer serve Bellum. We must escape together."

"How?" she said, practical as ever. "There is no way out of Bellum's stronghold only... only..." a voice was speaking to her at the back of her mind. "There is only one way," she said slowly. "We can only escape by trusting in Salvis."

Esram was not at all sure. "Well, at least I can get you out of this cell. But after that..."

"Salvis will help us," Morwen said firmly. "He has set us both free. If the King's son has set us free then we really are free and there is no such thing as failure."

In the gathering darkness, Petroc and Cherry crossed the Meadow of Flowers. When they reached the place where Lord Bellum had lost his crown, they stopped. The gloomy walls of the stronghold towered above them. Music and laughter reached their ears and they felt a chill of dread for they knew that the noise meant the feast was still going on. They also knew that when Bellum's banquets went on long into the night, he would be entertained by tormenting those servants who had upset him that day. Cherry had usually managed to keep out of trouble and escape his attention, but Petroc was summoned many times. Now, at the thought of going back inside the castle, all those terrible memories flooded back to him. They each admitted the fear to themselves, but not to each other.

"Wait," said Cherry. "It will help us if we stop for a little while and think of Lord Salvis."

Petroc sighed impatiently. "What good will that do?"

Even as he spoke, he realised that they were no longer alone. Slowly, he turned his head and saw that Lord Veritan was behind them.

Veritan looked long and hard at Petroc until the boy lowered his eyes, unable to meet his searching gaze. "Petroc, son of Tobias, why do you not ask the King for help? Why are you so proud?"

Petroc looked at his feet. He knew his face was red. "Well, even though you have not asked, the King is aware of your need for help. I have come to help you."

"Lord, there is only one of you," Cherry said tentively, "but there are many in Bellum's stronghold."

"One Lord of the Palace is a match for a thousand," Veritan told them quite sternly. "Even so, I cannot enter Bellum's house any more than he is able to enter the King's Palace." Cherry looked at Petroc. His face was scornful. She knew that he was thinking that when it came to a fight, Veritan was no more use than Salvis had been.

"What shall we do then, Lord?" she asked.

"Petroc, you must learn to trust the King," Veritan said almost angrily. "Do you think the King, who sent his own son to die in your place, would forsake you now?"

"I know the Lord would never leave us or forsake us," Cherry answered quietly.

"No, he would not, and I am going to help you, even though I cannot enter the castle."

118

* * *

Esram led Morwen along a dark, narrow tunnel, only just high enough for them to stand upright. A grown man would have to bend double. It stank of death and decay.

Morwen shuddered. "What is this used for, Esram?"

"You are best not to know."

In spite of her renewed love for Salvis, she began to feel afraid. Salvis did not banish fear, he gave strength to overcome it. How could she be sure that Esram was helping her and not leading her into a trap of his own? Then, she felt him squeeze her hand and she sensed the King's loving power in his touch. "Where does this lead, Esram?" she whispered.

"Ssh! You will see. You have to trust me."

Morwen had no choice. They came to a small door and Esram pushed it open, just wide enough to see out.

"Come. No-one is there. It is safe."

She held back. "There must be guards. Surely they would not leave any door unguarded?"

"They would this one!"

"Why?" Morwen began to feel afraid again. "Esram, what is this passage used for?"

Esram sighed. "Very well. Sometimes Bellum's prisoners die. Sometimes he has them killed. Sometimes they become sick and any who touch them may become sick too..."

"Sickness? You mean there is sickness here that takes lives?"

"Not in your cell. That is clean. But this is the way the bodies are taken from the castle to be burnt. We have to get out of here. We have to take the risk. There is no other way. Morwen, if Bellum finds you he will show you no mercy. Nor me either, now that I have helped you."

"But I only freed the butterflies! That is not so bad?"

"Oh, yes, it is! You do nothing, nothing to go against Lord Bellum."

"But outside, there must be people about. How shall we get out of the castle and across the moat?"

"One step at a time," said Esram. The truth was he did not know what they were going to do. "Morwen, we have to go!"

By this time she could see that there really was no other way, so they crept out into the growing darkness. All was quiet. The night air was heady after the stench of the passage. They were at the back of the castle, so, keeping well within the shadow of the castle walls, they moved quickly towards the gate.

At the first corner, they sensed danger, as they heard the sound of marching feet.

"I said there would be guards!" Morwen whispered, panic rising in her heart.

"Quick – in here!" He took her arm and roughly pulled her through a wooden door, shutting it behind them.

They were in a sort of barn with a small cart of hay and a tired-looking brown horse in a stable. Without ceremony, Esram picked her up and threw her on the cart, covering her completely in straw.

Morwen did not need to ask what the cart was used for. It would be the way dead prisoners left the castle.

"Keep still and be quiet!" he hissed tersely.

The footsteps stopped at the door and Esram slipped outside. She heard him speak to the guards. There was loud laughter. It was horrible, mocking and cruel.

"If that maiden knew what Lord Bellum has planned for her, she would die of fear," shouted a man's voice. Esram laughed too, then said, "Your duty is finished now. You must come and watch. I am on my way to fetch the maid from the cells. Shall I warn her what is in store?"

"No, let it be a surprise! We shall enjoy it more!"

There was more laughter and then the sound of marching feet and Esram went back inside the barn and very gently helped Morwen to sit up.

"They have gone. And this has given me an idea. The new guard will not be aware of what has happened tonight, because they would not be allowed to join in the feast. If you hide in the cart I should be able to drive right across the drawbridge. They will think..." his voice tailed off.

Morwen pulled straw from her mouth.

"They will think I am a dead prisoner," she finished for him. "Esram, is it really the only way?"

"I believe so."

She held out her hands. "At least free me from these chains first? They are hurting me. My wrists are bleeding."

"No. We do not have time. We must go now or not at all."

Even as he spoke, he was harnessing the horse to the cart. Then, he made her lie down and covered her from head to foot with a heavy blanket.

It was very dark beneath the blanket. Her heart

was banging so hard she thought she would be heard. All she could do was to cry silently to Salvis. "Salvis, Salvis, please help me. Please..."

The cart rumbled away and then stopped. Once again she heard laughter, the same cruel laughter.

"Ho, Esram, not another dead?"

"Only one little one!"

"Let me see."

Morwen stopped breathing for what seemed like an eternity until she heard Esram call back.

"Not this time, friend. This one's sickly from top to toe!"

"Oh well, best go then. We do not want to catch it!"

Morwen clearly heard the sound of the draw-bridge being lowered and the cart rocked from side to side as it moved on to the wooden planks.

"Please Salvis, please... please ..."

They must have been half-way across the bridge when a roar like an angry lion reached their ears.

Bellum had discovered that Morwen was gone from her cell.

"You dare to defy me?" he bellowed. "Esram, come back here and bring that maid! Do as I say! Guard, stop them. Raise the drawbridge! Now!"

The bridge tilted upwards. The frightened horse reared. The cart jolted back. Morwen heard a roaring in her ears as it overturned and both she and Esram were thrown into the icy, black water of the moat.

Morwen's breath was forced out of her lungs by the sudden cold and shock. She tried to swim, but her long skirts and the heavy chains pulled her down beneath the water. Just as she was about to lose consciousness she felt strong arms beneath her. Her head was raised above the water and Esram swam for them both until they reached the other side.

Eager hands helped pull them out. They lay still for a few minutes, oblivious to Bellum's roaring, and when they opened their eyes it was to see Petroc and Cherry bending over them.

They were helped to their feet and first Cherry, then Petroc, gave Morwen a hug. She was astonished to see tears in Petroc's eyes.

"Esram, he helped me escape. He has joined the King."

Petroc nodded, not sure of what to believe.

"You seem to be for ever pulling one of us out of the water, Esram. We are in your debt."

"Look!" cried Cherry. "Look at Lord Veritan!"

The drawbridge had been lowered again and Bellum stood ready to cross, but the Lord of the Palace was standing facing him. Veritan's golden sword was drawn and he was swinging it from side to side in a glorious display of flashing light. Bellum could roar all he liked, but there was no way he could pass by him.

Veritan called mockingly to the King's enemy. "Bellum! Another failure! You will never defeat the King!"

"You have no right on my land, Veritan!" Bellum's voice was full of hatred.

"I have not been on your land," Veritan laughed. "I did not need to. You could not even get the better of two children."

Now Lord Bellum's voice changed from that of a roaring lion to a hissing serpent.

"Then go, all of you! But mark me, I have not

finished with them yet! I will not be defied by anyone!"

With that he turned and stormed back inside the castle.

In the sudden unexpected silence, Petroc hugged his sister and for the first time noticed her appearance. "Morwen, what in all the world are you wearing? Oh, what have they done to you? How could they put you in chains?"

As he spoke, without anyone moving, Morwen's chains fell away of their own accord. No one touched them.

The four children looked at each other in disbelief and Morwen stared down at her hands. "It must be Salvis," she breathed. "Salvis has set me free. Look, look over there."

In a flash of light they saw a tall, slim man dressed in grey standing a little way from them. As they watched, he waved his hand in a salute and was gone. They knew it was Salvis; even Esram knew that no one else could bring such peace.

Now that Bellum had gone, Veritan came over to them.

"Do not be afraid, little ones. The King's power is greater by far than Bellum's could ever be. The King is a giant and Bellum is no bigger than a worm. Just a worm! Petroc, you did not have to go inside the castle, but you were willing to go. The King knew that. Trust always in the King and then Bellum cannot hurt you."

Veritan left them quickly, now that his work was done. Laughing and crying and too exhausted to talk, they began to make their way across the Meadow of Flowers into the safety of the Dark Forest and home.

Chapter 17

...is Free Indeed

The light of first dawn was filtering through the shutters of the farmhouse windows when Petroc woke up the next morning.

Next to him, Esram was still asleep and snoring loudly. Petroc frowned, for he was still not sure whether Carrik's nephew was really a friend.

Amos was not there. He must have got up early. Quietly, so he did not disturb Esram, Petroc slipped out from between the hay and the covering of furs that were his bedding. His bare feet touched the cold stone floor and, shivering as he picked up his boots, he tiptoed away.

Once outside the house, he pulled on his boots. Amos was standing by the farm gate staring over the fields, now sown with good corn, the three scarecows flapping in the breeze. A low mist hung over the ground and over the distant hills, telling them that the Time of Snows would soon be here.

His uncle did not turn round but continued to stare ahead at the land as Petroc joined him.

"You know that Carrik will not let things rest here?" Amos said quietly.

"Yes," Petroc admitted, "That is what I wanted to talk to you about. Do you think that he is really loyal to the King?"

"Esram? Yes... yes, I do... He does have the

King's peace in his heart."

"Oh, the King, the King," Petroc cried. "It is bad enough that the girls talk in this way but I had thought better of you. You are a grown-up, Uncle Amos. You must see this is just a children's tale?"

Amos said nothing. He did not have to. Petroc had always been taught to respect his elders.

"I should not have been rude to you, I'm sorry for that," he said, but his voice did not sound very sorry. "You are my mother's brother and she would not want me to be so rude... But I am more interested in protecting the farm than in the King's peace or the King's power or whatever it is called!"

"Maybe," Amos said mildly, "the King's power is what we need to protect the farm? Now, as for Esram, the only danger he brings to us is from his Uncle Carrik. He will have his heart set on revenge. Come, let us walk before breakfast."

They strode off together, the big, red-haired man with the loud voice and the tall, red-haired boy who was so quiet, of the same family, yet with such different ways.

Amos led the way to High Hill and as they walked, they spoke of family matters, of Tobias and Martha and Delfi, who was part of the family now. They spoke of Morwen too, the sister that Petroc had so nearly lost. Amos spoke to him as a man, not a child, realising that the things that had happened to him during the last year had not been children's things. His childhood days had ended when he had been taken off to serve Carrik, his enemy. Last night he had overcome his fear and been willing to go right into Lord Bellum's castle. Amos would not insult Petroc by treating him as a child.

High Hill was shrouded in mist, and the grass was wet with dew. They sat down in a place where, on a clear day, they would have been able to see most of the island of Karensa. Today, swirling white tendrils obscured their view beyond the Dark Forest, even though the sun was trying to break through the clouds.

"Why is the mist always there?" Petroc asked, suddenly curious.

"The time of year, of course. You know that in the Time of Gathering we always have misty mornings."

"No, I don't mean that. I mean the mist over the sea. Why are we never allowed to see the world beyond the mist?"

Amos frowned. "No one really knows why. The King must have a reason for the mist being there."

They sat in silence for a while, each with their own thoughts. Petroc was remembering Luke and Rosie. What was their world like? He knew it was very different from Karensa. He would like to see it for himself.

As the sun rose higher and the mist thinned, they saw them! Riders on horseback led by Carrik. Each man carried a flare in his hand.

Petroc's heart was pounding with anger and with fear. "Uncle Amos, we must get back to the farm! Carrik is set to destroy it again!"

"Yes, we must get back," Amos agreed. "We must get back because Esram and the girls are on their own."

Morwen snuggled down deeper beneath her covering of furs and let her mind roam freely over the events of the day before.

She had thought she would never see this farm again and she would never forget the feeling of being locked in that cold cell with no hope of escape. She had learnt a hard lesson, but being friends with Salvis again made it almost worthwhile. Almost. And Esram, asleep on the other side of the curtain with Petroc and Amos – who would ever have thought that Esram would become one of them?

Morwen liked Esram more than she cared to admit and she knew that he liked her. She remembered the way they had danced together and how gentle he had been as he taught her the steps. He was not like Carrik at all, and if he had been cruel to Petroc and Cherry when they were in Bellum's castle, then he had changed now. He had once risked his life to save Petroc from the sea at Black Rock Bay. Now he had risked his life to save her.

She could not remember much about what had happened when they had finally got home last night, but she knew that some of their friends were there to meet them, and someone had found her some proper clothes to wear. She recalled that Cherry had helped her wash and change and then put her to bed on clean, sweet hay. The green silk gown had been taken away and burnt, for they wanted nothing here that belonged to Bellum's house. New clothes had been found for Esram, too, and his silver tunic ended its days with the green gown on a fire in the yard.

Morwen tried to get up quietly, but she could not help waking Cherry and that woke Esram, and soon they were all up.

Amos and Petroc were missing, so Morwen decided to start breakfast. Cherry went to fetch fresh milk from the goat and Morwen began to make a huge bowl of creamy porridge. Esram did not seem to have any experience of cooking, so for today, he watched what Morwen was doing.

"How do you feel?" she asked.

Esram shook his head. "I do not know. Yesterday I was a lord in a castle. Now I am a farm boy who has never worked on a farm."

"But you do have the King's peace in your heart?"

"Yes, oh yes. But who is there to believe me? I shall always be hated by your people as the King's enemy."

"It will take a long while," Morwen agreed. "But in time people will know you and believe that... What is that?"

Cherry ran in from the yard. "Carrik!" she gasped. "Carrik is here! He is coming up to the farm!"

They all rushed outside and, as always, it was Morwen who was the practical one.

"Esram, you must hide. It will be you they've come for. We will stay here to meet them. Oh, where are Petroc and Amos?"

Esram did as he was told and the two girls clung tightly together as the riders lined up in the yard. There was no doubt as to what they intended to do.

Morwen and Cherry were very afraid, yet they tried not to show their fear. What could two young girls do against a group of armed men?

Carrik called down to them. "So, you find the farm more attractive than a castle, Morwen? Well

129

I do not care about that, it is your choice and you will suffer for it, but where is Esram? Where is my nephew? What have you done to him?"

"Nothing at all, Uncle Carrik." Esram came out of hiding. "I came of my own free will. I am a follower of Salvis now."

Carrik sneered, "Then you will be a follower of Salvis with no roof over your head, for this one is about to go up in flames." He laughed loudly. "Once again! Was it hard work to rebuild it, Morwen? You should not have bothered. It will be gone again in an hour. Was it worth it?"

"Wait!" Amos cut across Carrik as he and Petroc ran across the yard. "I will not let you do this, Carrik! This farm belongs to my sister, Martha, and her family now."

"No, Amos." Morwen remembered how Tobias had died defending the farm. She would not see her uncle suffer the same end. To her, the farm was not worth such a high price.

Petroc did not agree. Once before, he had sacrificed himself for his friend Luke. Now he did the same thing again for his father's farm.

"It is me who Bellum wants," he said firmly. He stood in front of Carrik's horse. "He wants me to go back to him of my own free will. Leave the farm alone, and leave the girls alone. I promise I will return with you and shall not try to escape, ever. You will be in favour with Bellum for the rest of your days. Take me, Carrik, and leave the farm. Bellum shall have what he desires."

His face was very white as he dropped to his knees in front of Carrik's horse.

This was the last thing Carrik had expected. He

hesitated, and in that split second, with a mighty crash of thunder, the sky was plunged into darkness.

After the thunder came lightning and with the lightning came rain, but such rain as they had never seen before. At once, the flares they had brought to set fire to the farm were put out by the torrent, and the yard turned to mud beneath their feet. Then, there was more thunder, and in this thunder it seemed as though a voice spoke, a voice that held all the fury of creation as the wind had done, the day Bellum lost his crown in the Meadow of Flowers.

The children clung to Amos in fear, as rain splashed from the roof and water streamed across the land. This was no ordinary storm. It was a storm commanded by the King himself in his anger. Carrik's men had fled, their horses neighing wildly. Then, as suddenly as it had begun, the storm ceased and daylight returned.

Carrik was looking round him in fear when his horse threw him and fled, leaving him crawling on his knees in the mud.

They watched in horror and then amazement as his hands clawed the soft ground. His eyes were rolling wildly. Suddenly he threw himself full length in the mud.

"This King really is King!" he shouted. "None other could command the wind and the rain! Salvis, you really are the King's son! You are Lord! There is none other like you! Forgive me, Lord! I have turned from you in so many ways! I have persecuted your followers. Be my Lord! I turn away from Bellum and all he stands for."

As he spoke, the sun came out, and the heat made clouds of steam rise from their wet clothes.

"Who the Son sets free, is free indeed," said Morwen quietly.

Chapter 18

Butterfly Song

News of the strange storm quickly spread and very soon all their friends came to the farmhouse to find out what had really happened.

When they heard how the King had saved the farm from being burnt down by sending such rain, and how Carrik had forsaken Bellum and made Salvis his Lord, they wanted to meet together to praise their mighty King.

So, just as they had met many times before, they gathered in Petroc's house to give thanks. Many were uneasy about Carrik and Esram, finding it hard to believe that they could really trust them after all the bad things they had done, and so these two sat alone in a corner of the room while the others sang songs of praise to Salvis and to his father the King.

Today was unlike the other times. Today, as their songs rose up, they all became very aware of Salvis himself being there with them. They could not see him, but each person knew that he was there as they felt his peace flowing through them and over them.

Only one thing spoilt Morwen's happiness today; Petroc still refused to believe. He was gracious enough not to stop them from using his house for their meeting, yet he sat by Morwen's side like a lump of stone, refusing to join in the singing. He seemed very unhappy about the way things were going as the sense of the King's son being with them grew stronger and stronger with each song of praise.

Morwen looked over to Cherry, but Cherry was so lost in thinking of Salvis that she did not see her. A strange thought came into Morwen's mind. It did not come from her. She believed Salvis may have put it there.

She slipped from her place and tip-toed up to Amos and Raldi who were leading the meeting.

Amos bent his head down so Morwen could whisper in his ear.

"Uncle Amos, I think Salvis wants to heal Cherry's foot."

The two men looked at each other and then back to her.

"It is a long way to the King's Palace,"Amos whispered back. "It would take many hours to get her there. We cannot go today. Perhaps another time?"

"No. I believe Salvis wants to heal her and we do not have to go to the King's Palace." Morwen was getting agitated.

Raldi saw how she was feeling.

He said, "The maiden could be right. We cannot ignore this. What shall we do?"

"I know what to do," Morwen said quickly. "I saw Salvis do it many times when we were all living at the Bay of Dolphins. Please let me try."

"Is it what you really feel, child?" Amos asked kindly.

"Yes," she nodded. "I can hear Salvis speaking into my heart."

"She should try," Raldi decided and he called Cherry out to the front.

Cherry looked worried. "What have I done?" she said, as she stood before the whole company.

Morwen smiled, feeling a sudden rush of love for her. How could she have been so jealous? The thought of it now made her ashamed and silently she asked Salvis to forgive her again. She told Cherry what she felt Salvis wanted to do.

"Would you let me try? Are you willing?" she asked.

Cherry began to tremble. "I do want Salvis to make me better. What do I have to do?"

"Nothing," Morwen told her, remembering what Salvis had done in the past. "You never knew Salvis like we did, but think about him now. Think about how he died and took away the punishment for all our disobedience when Karensa turned away from the King."

"All right then. I am willing."

As Cherry closed her eyes, Morwen knelt down and placed her hands on the damaged foot. There was a sudden hush in the room as everyone joined Morwen in quietly asking the King for Cherry to be healed.

"Please, Lord King," she began. "Please make this foot well again. We don't want Cherry to hurt any more." Then, she grew more confident. "Lord King, you healed people through Salvis and we have his peace in our hearts. You have given us your power. Show us how to use it like Salvis did. Heal her now, Lord, please."

"Is that it?" Cherry asked, feeling embarrassed and glad that it was over. Her foot felt very warm.

Morwen nodded, disappointed that nothing seemed to have happened. How could she ever have thought that she could do the work of Salvis? Who did she think she was?

As Cherry turned to go back to her place, a cry arose from the people. The limp had gone!

Cherry began to laugh and cry at the same time. "It does not hurt any more! I can walk as well as you now! Morwen, oh Morwen you have done it! Thank you, thank you!"

"Not me," Morwen said hastily. "Thank the King not me, Cherry. He made you well. All I did was ask."

Then she too began to cry, but this time it was with joy. It was true! They did have the King's power!

Everyone began to praise the King saying how great he was and thanking him for giving his son, Salvis, to save the people of Karensa. They praised him as never before.

Except for Petroc. Petroc walked out of the room.

Morwen followed him. He was walking so fast that she had to run to keep up with him and it was like that all the way to High Hill to the very spot where he had sat with Amos that morning.

Morwen struggled for breath.

"Petroc, why do you hate Salvis?" she gasped at last. "You were always loyal to the King."

"I don't hate the King," Petroc replied, staring straight ahead across the sea.

"Then why won't you accept that Salvis is Lord of Karensa and ask him to fill you with his peace?"

"Oh, Salvis, Salvis! If it is not the King, it is Salvis! Salvis is dead. I saw him die in Bellum's stronghold! It was his ghost that we saw later on the beach!"

"It was not a ghost! He lifted me up in his arms. A ghost could not do that! He was real!"

"Then where is he now?"

"You know where. Back in the King's Palace. That is why the King sent the new power to us. Oh Petroc, please, why will you not ask him to be Lord of your life?"

"I have done, but nothing happened!" Petroc shouted angrily. He had never told anyone that before.

Morwen was at a loss for words. Salvis would never refuse anyone, she knew that. Something must be wrong.

"Maybe you did not ask properly," she said lamely.

Then all at once, Petroc understood. He had asked Salvis into his life many times, but it had always been on his own terms. He had not wanted Salvis to change any part of his life. He had not allowed him to take away his anger and hatred and he had not been willing to forgive Carrik or even Esram. He still wanted to hate the people that had hurt him in the past. He had to let go of his hatred, even of the man who had killed his father. Salvis had no room in his own heart for hatred and he expected those who would follow him to forgive, just as he did...

To his dismay, he felt tears run down his face as he realised his own hardness of heart. His father would not be pleased with his efforts to rebuild the farm because he had done it for the wrong reasons. In a torrent of love and shame, the hatred left him and was gone for ever, swept away by the immense love of the King's son.

"Lord, please forgive me. Help me to forgive and forget too. Be my own Lord for ever."

"Petroc," Morwen whispered through her own tears, "Petroc, he is here. The Lord is here."

This time, he really was there, standing behind them by a clump of yellow gorse, looking just as they had last seen him on the beach, and his kind brown eyes were still so full of love for them. Such love had to be felt to be believed. It was beyond human understanding.

"Petroc, it has been such a long time," he said gently.

Petroc and Morwen fell on their knees before him. It felt like the right place to be.

"I cannot stay long with you," he told them. "As you see me now, is not really how I am. If I were to appear to you as I really am, your hearts would fail you and you would die of fear. My true place now is in the King's Palace at his side. Yet I have come because I have things that I delight to tell you. Come and sit with me and listen; listen well."

Petroc and Morwen sat on the hillside with Salvis and they listened carefully as the King's son continued to speak to them in that same gentle voice that held eternal peace, sharing secrets with them never before told. Both brother and sister lost all track of time as they listened intently.

"And finally," said Salvis after some time, "I have work for you to do. Petroc, the King made it possible for you to restore your farm and now that you are obedient to him, he has a purpose for it. You are to make it a special place where all those who follow me, rich or poor, are always made welcome."

"Yes Lord, it will be so."

"Now, for Carrik and Esram I have other work. Let them stay with you for a while and learn about me, and when they have learnt, they must go to teach the people on the far side of the island, for those people do not really understand why I came. You must be sure to tell Carrik this."

Suddenly Petroc was curious again about other lands.

"Salvis," he said, "what about the world beyond the mist? What about Luke's world? Do the people there know about you?"

"In that world," Salvis replied very seriously, "one Man gave up his own life to pay the price for every wrong thing that anyone has ever done. This Man was innocent and did not deserve to die, so he now lives again and anyone who is really sorry for their sins can turn to him and be forgiven. Then he will give them a new start and fill each heart with his peace. He is the Son of the Greatest King Ever, and he has a special name before which, one day, every knee must bow. This true story is told in a very special book called the Bible."

Petroc was pleased with this, pleased that Luke and Rosie were not on their own in the world beyond the mist.

"What of me, Lord?" Morwen murmured. "I know I was foolish and turned away from you, but I will never again."

"Morwen, you were always close to my heart when we lived in the cave house and you are still dear to me, because you of all people understand me. You have been foolish and listened to Lord Bellum when he whispered wrong thoughts in your ear. Learn from your disobedience, my child, and see that you learn well. You found it was easy to enter the Castle of Shadows, but only the King could get you out."

"Yes, Lord, I have learnt that. I will not go back again."

"Do not make rash promises, child. All flesh is weak. You must continue to learn how to live in the King's power as you have done today when the King healed your friend's foot. Encourage others to have your faith. Let your heart become gentle again, as it was long ago. And do not look so upset, for believe me, you will learn, and then the King has a great work for you to do. Until then, live under your brother's authority. Help him and give him your support. You, Petroc, be kind to your sister as you were in the days before the war. You must both help Esram too, and Cherry." Morwen felt her cheeks burn as she remembered her jealousy.

"Petroc, you once wanted to touch me to make sure I was alive. Do so now," Salvis continued.

"Lord... I... I cannot!" Petroc exclaimed. "I want to believe without touching you!"

"Well done! Now, I must leave. No, do not weep for you shall see me again. One day you will come to live with me in the King's Palace, but until then you each have work to do."

He placed his hands over each of their heads in turn and then he was gone.

Morwen opened her eyes. Petroc smiled down at her and she knew that once more he was the brother she loved. They stood together, brother and

140

sister, at peace with each other after such a long time. "So much has happened in a year, Petroc," Morwen sighed.

"Much has happened since we met Luke and Rosie. Look at the mist, Morwen, does it never move?"

"Once it did, when you were not here. There is a land not far away, a land where Luke and Rosie live."

"Perhaps we shall see them again soon," said Petroc.

"I hope so!" said Morwen as she drew close to him and linked her arm in his. "We have so much to tell them."

"I want to tell Luke about meeting Salvis today." said Petroc, his voice full of awe. From this moment on, no matter what happened to him in his life, whether good or bad, if he should prosper or if he should die, there would never be another day like this day, for on this day the King's own son had come to him and forgiven him and made him his own.

As they stood together, the butterflies returned and flocked round them.

"It's as though Salvis told them, to come and thank you for setting them free from the Castle of Shadows!"

Then, Morwen began to sing in words older than time and sweeter than tomorrow's dawn, secret words of ancient days, words of power and great beauty. Soon, Petroc joined in.

The notes rose and fell, and rose again on the breeze, mingling with the gentle song of the butterflies.

THE END OF THE BEGINNING

Look out for the next book in the Tales of Karensa *series...*

Children of the Second Morning
Jean Cullop

Rosie hesitated by the wooden door. "Luke, think! If we go through there we may not be able to get back! At least not for ages. Remember last time. We were on Karensa for nearly a year. Think of the dangers, Luke! Think of sleeping on straw mattresses! Think of boring food and no telly, and work instead of school... and there are other dangers on Karensa. Think about Bellum!"

Luke closed his eyes, trying to make sense of his thoughts. Karensa was calling him. Salvis was calling him. It was like going home. The call on his life was strong and he couldn't deny it.

He felt Salvis close to them, so close that he could almost feel his great heart beating. Just to be there, on Karensa again... The call became stronger and stronger.

Luke walked through the door, and Rosie went with him now, slipping her hand trustingly in his, just as she had done when she climbed into the boat with him the first time.

The door closed behind them, and when they looked, the door and the stone wall had gone. They were alone in a strange land but as they stood hand in hand, Poldawn faded away to a memory and Karensa became reality.

ISBN 1 85999 526 8

The first book in the Tales of Karensa *series...*

Where Dolphins race with Rainbows
Jean Cullop

"Welcome to Karensa."

Luke opened his eyes, blinking against the strong sunlight. He was sprawled on his back on soft, dry sand. In front of him the sea was calm and deepest blue, the waves lapping gently against the shore.

So the mist and the storm were a dream? He was safely back at Poldawn.

But as he struggled to sit up he realised that there had been no dream. This was not Poldawn. This was a bay of clean, flat sand surrounded by cliffs, lush with flowering plants and bushes unlike anything he had ever imagined.

What was more, he was being watched by a group of the strangest looking people he had ever seen.

They all had long hair. The men wore theirs loose to their shoulders but the women and girls' hair was braided into several plaits and decorated with coloured ribbon. Men and women were dressed alike in long belted tunics, loose trousers and soft boots.

Stories of desert islands and cannibals flicked across Luke's mind.

"Welcome to Karensa," the voice repeated as one of the men came and knelt by Luke's side on the sand. He reached out his hand and touched Luke's wet T-shirt and shorts and clipped hair and the boy suddenly realised that he looked as strange to these people as they did to him.

ISBN 1 85999 383 4